Even Still

Jenn Faulk

ISBN:1492979910
ISBN-13:9781492979913

CONTENTS

ACKNOWLEDGMENTS

To those who know the anticipation of coming "in view of a call." To those who have ever taken a church directory home so as to memorize each and every name and face. To those who have heard the sermon three times before he ever stood at the pulpit and preached it. To those who were expected to have all the answers when they didn't even know there were any questions. To those who know Sunday morning begins on Saturday night in the parsonage. To those who have prayed over a tired, broken man after a hard deacons' meeting. To those who have celebrated seeing lives forever changed because the Word of God has been preached.

To those who love much because they are loved much, by Christ Himself.

This is for you, sweet pastors' wives.

CHAPTER ONE

Abby

Abby was waiting for the vomit to begin and end so that she could get on with her life.

It was Preview Weekend, and she was getting a preview of idiocy on a grander scale than any she could have anticipated years earlier, back when she'd first heard about the small college. She'd already committed to attending the university, already knew everything she honestly needed to know about going there the next fall, and already had an idea about what dorm life would be like. But Rachel, her best friend, had pleaded with her to come that weekend for one more look into the near future that would be theirs.

Abby sincerely doubted that her future would include any time spent with Grant, Rachel's brother, and his roommate, Seth, both of whom were attempting the gallon challenge in a room full of giggling girls and the handful of guys who kept cheering them on.

It was likely impossible for anyone to consume an entire gallon of milk in one hour without vomiting, but that didn't stop the two guys from enthusiastically attempting it. Again and again.

"Grant's already tried this a few times before," Rachel whispered, her eyes never leaving Seth, even as he wiped his forehead and put his hand to his stomach, swearing to his laughing friends that he was fine. "Last time, he got it all down in fifty-eight minutes… but threw up on the last drink."

"Doesn't count then, does it?," Abby asked, refraining from rolling her eyes at the juvenile (and stupid) game.

"Nope," Rachel grinned. "But I think Seth can do it."

Only because Rachel thought Seth could rope the moon and raise the dead, likely. This particular Preview Weekend had nothing to do with school for Rachel but everything to do with Seth, who she had sworn she would marry from the first day she met him years earlier when he became Grant's roommate. She and Abby had been best friends even then, and Abby could well remember the gushing that followed Rachel's deliriously exuberant text about Grant's new friend. They must have spent over three hours that weekend alone and countless hours since discussing how Rachel could get Seth to notice her. Her attraction bordered on obsession, her admiration neared delusion, and as Abby surveyed Rachel's intended target with a critical eye… well, she couldn't figure out why Rachel cared so much, even if he was cute enough, loved Jesus, and seemed to be a nice guy. He certainly wasn't worth the gushing Rachel was doing, as he let out a wet-sounding belch, then held his hand to his mouth, and said, "That does *not* disqualify me!"

"He's awesome," Rachel murmured.

Abby sighed. "He's about to spew milk all over this room, and –"

She stopped short as her gaze fell on another person who seemed as bored by the scene before them as she was. He was sitting on the fringes of the crowd, frowning over at Grant and Seth both. Dark hair, lighter eyes, and… he caught her staring at him. She met his gaze for a long, calm moment, then glanced at Rachel... then looked right back over at him.

4

He was still watching her.

"Who's that?," she asked Rachel.

Rachel followed her gaze. "Oh, that's Seth's brother. Stuart." She lowered her voice as she raised her eyebrows. "He's a real *drag*."

"How so?," Abby asked, even as Stuart sighed and looked back to his brother, glancing at his watch for a moment.

"Just super serious," Rachel shrugged, "and a real killjoy. Going all big brother on Grant and Seth a lot of the time, making them study and all, you know. Surprised he hasn't broken up the gallon challenge yet."

"Hmm," Abby murmured, even as Stuart looked back over at her appraisingly. "He sounds boring."

"Yeah."

"But he's hotter than Seth," she said appreciatively.

Rachel gasped at this. Actually gasped at it. "No one's hotter than Seth."

"Yeah, well," Abby said, noting that only a tiny amount of milk was left in both gallons. This was the time to leave the room so as to avoid seeing the gore and carnage. "Hey, I'm going to slip out for a second."

"Where are you going?," Rachel asked. "You're about to miss –"

"Yeah, that's why I'm slipping out," she answered. "I'm heading to the restroom back in our wonderful hostesses' room –"

"Why in the world?," Rachel rolled her eyes. "Those two girls make Stuart look like fun –"

And with that, Grant threw up, and Abby rushed out, eyes covered.

Stu

Seth? Was an idiot.

Stu watched as his brother scrambled to get away from his roommate's puke, covering his own mouth with his hand, even as he clung to the nearly-finished gallon of milk. One more sip and he was likely a goner himself. Stu was certain it would come to pass and sighed at the waste of energy, time, and intelligence. Seth's and his own.

But this was life. Stu had been watching out for Seth for... well, forever. Stu was the fourth son born to his mother, not special or out of the ordinary in any way, apart from the fact that his arrival preceded Seth's, who was born too early and had the entire family worried as he struggled in the NICU. Stu had been a baby himself and had no recollection of that stressful time in their lives, but he, more than the others, had been affected by it in the long run. Every day since Seth had been brought home from the hospital, Stu had been admonished by his mother to watch out for the baby, to take care of him, to be his "big, strong, older brother."

Stu had taken the job very seriously as a child. And old habits? Never die, no matter how much Stu wished he could just flippin' not care about the dumb things his younger brother, now a grown man, felt inclined to do.

The milk wasn't really the problem tonight, though. No, the problem tonight was the pretty underage girl staring at Seth with unabashed adoration, even as he finally spewed.

Stu knew better than Seth when it came to things like this.

"Stu!," the girl shrieked as Seth coughed and wiped his mouth before lying back on the floor with a grimace. "Seth needs something to keep hydrated! Do you know where we can find something for him to drink?"

"Rachel," he sighed, knowing her name and very nearly everything about her after these past three years of her throwing herself at his brother, "do you really think it's wise to put something back on his stomach after that?"

She bit her lip as she smoothed Seth's hair back with her hand. "Well…"

"I don't think he needs anything to drink," Stu said. "The man has had enough as it is."

"I'm just worried about him," she said, cradling Seth's head in her lap, while her own brother laid on the floor, totally ignored, moaning and clutching his stomach. "He threw up a lot!"

Stu stood and walked over to Grant, kicking him lightly. "You okay, man?"

"I think I'm going to die," Grant groaned.

"Likely so," Stu murmured. "Why don't you go sit out in the hall and get some fresh air? Looks like Seth's about to –"

And he did. Again. Very nearly missing the trash can that Rachel threw under his mouth at the last possible minute.

"I'll stay here with Seth," Rachel cooed. "I'm going to be a nursing student next year, you know. Good practice and all. I'll take such good care of him."

Stu didn't doubt that she'd try.

He frowned as he pulled Grant up by the arms, cursing the responsibility he felt for both idiots now, after introducing them to college life three years ago when they arrived as wide-eyed freshmen.

Back then, Stu had been a confident, smooth-talking upperclassman who had ushered the two boys into the big middle of his messy, wild life. Drinking, lots of drinking, rowdy parties, and too many girls. Stu had been on a straight and narrow path before college began, but those first few years at the university had done a work on him.

He hadn't always been that way. He'd come to the university with a good head on his shoulders and a big life plan laid out before him. Law school, politics, becoming someone besides the fourth son born to a family so big that even his own mother called him by the wrong name half the time – this was Stu's plan. He'd jumped in with both feet, joining campus organizations that would get him closer to his goal, finding the best opportunities to network, and finding, along the way, that his gift for speaking frankly and seeing people for who they really were made him something of a rarity in a fake world. In no time at all, he could see how easy people were to manipulate, to sway, to win over, and before he knew it, he was Mr. Charisma, well on his way to winning every popular vote out there.

Stu had felt little conviction about how this had changed him until the weekend that Seth and Grant arrived for freshman orientation. He took them out, proud to let his little brother see just what kind of big man he'd become here in this place where no one knew that there were a whole horde of other Huntington brothers. It was a place where guys liked to drink with him, people listened when he spoke, and every girl wanted to go home with him. He brought the two, wide-eyed, innocent freshmen into this world he had created for himself without a nagging doubt or concern that it was in any way wrong or harmful to them.

Grant was quickly and effectively smashed after just a few beers. Stu hardly even noticed, intent as he was on working the room and reconnecting with people who had just come back from the summer away. He was halfway to a pleasant buzz himself and was considering which of the three clearly interested women who had been trailing him all evening would be invited up to his room with him later.

And Seth? Seth had watched it all with horror, an untouched beer in his hand and shock on his face.

"Stu," he whispered. "Is this what... you do?"

Stu gave his brother a smile. "This is college, Seth. This is what everyone does." Then quietly, with a laugh, "Mom's not here to find out, man."

Seth looked down, then up at his brother again, actual tears in his eyes. "Wasn't Mom I was worried about. I didn't think you were like this."

There was disappointment there. And judgment. They were from a religious family, and most of the brothers drank the Kool-Aid with conviction and celebration. But not Stu. Because he knew what real life was now that he was in college, and Jesus and PG living and acting like it all mattered two thousand years after the fact was stupid.

"Just having fun," Stu said. "Time to grow up, little man."

"It's time for me to go back to my dorm," Seth had said, hurt in his eyes. "And to get Grant –" he indicated his passed out roommate – "back as well."

Grant was lying in a heap on the couch. "Oh, he's fine," Stu said, slipping his arms around the girls who were leading him away even as Seth blushed at them.

"Stuart," Seth had said severely. "Grant's dad is one of the academic deans."

And this? Had snapped Stu out of the mellowed out buzz he found himself in. He had plans to go on from here and make a name for himself, and killing the dean's son during his undergraduate career? Would certainly lose him some votes somewhere along the way.

So, he and Seth had gotten Grant back to the safety of the dorm where they'd thrown him in bed and propped him up so he wouldn't choke on his own vomit. And Seth had turned to Stu, with an icy expression and a chill in his voice, sniffing back tears, and said, "I don't want to hang out with you here if this is the kind of thing you're into."

9

Stu had rolled his eyes, annoyed by the holier than thou act he was getting. "Breakin' my heart, Seth," he said. "Not like I want to hang out with you anyway. Pathetic crybaby."

"Maybe I am a crybaby," Seth had said softly, "but at least I'm not a loser like you. Trying to act like you're all confident and secure in who you are, but you're not. And you look stupid, Stu."

"You're stupid," Stu offered lamely, making a face at him.

"Proving my point," Seth said. "And I *know* who I am in Christ. And I'm not ever going to be like you."

And maybe there had been some truth in it. But Stu had wandered off that night, trying his best to ignore all that Seth said.

It wasn't until a month later, when he saw Seth at another party, that he reconsidered what had been said. Seth, with all of his security in who he was in Christ, was apparently having a harder time standing by his convictions this far into the semester than he had figured he would. Stu could see that he was drunk. And Stu himself was stone cold sober enough to see that his innocent, virginal, little brother, who loved Jesus and had spent the majority of high school swearing to stay pure despite the struggles he had with his thought life and all the temptations around him, was just about to fall into a pit so large he couldn't claw his way out of it when one particular girl made her way over to him, sat in his lap, and lowered her lips to his.

Stu had recognized her instantly because he himself had been with her the week before.

And for the first time, Stu saw what he had probably looked like back when he started college and realized that in no time at all, Seth would be him... a man who had grown to despise women apart from what he could get from them, who drank alone because he drank all the time, and who found no greater purpose in life than himself.

A man who had no god or convictions at all.

Stuart Huntington didn't even want to be Stuart Huntingon... and he sure wasn't going to let Seth turn into him either.

So, despite the loud, drunken protests of his younger brother, Stu dragged him back to the dorm, telling him all the way there to shut up, and then forced him to stay put. And he was there in the morning when Seth woke up with his first and only hangover, assuring him that things had gone no farther than kissing with that girl, and promising him that they were going to turn things around.

They were *both* going to turn things around.

And they did.

But more than his actions had changed. He had gone back to what he had believed before coming to the university, found a church that taught as richly and deeply as the church of his childhood had, and believed it all, as a rational, redeemed adult. Finally.

He could thank his brother for the prompting and the nudging back to the straight and narrow... but Christ alone could be thanked for the heart change and the total transformation of Stuart Huntington.

The life plan changed. Stu wasn't going to make a name for himself. He was going to make a name for Christ and change the world for Him. Law theory, politics – pursuing this for Christ and His purposes.

It had been a big change.

What hadn't changed, however, was that Stu still felt the need, even now that he was in graduate school, to come back here and look out for his brother, who was, in the truest sense, his brother in Christ now, as they spurred one another on, kept one another accountable, and lived for Someone more than themselves.

He dropped Grant off in the hallway, made sure he was upright, then went back in to Seth so as to keep an eye on Rachel, who would probably stoop so low as to try and seduce a vomiting man.

And he wondered, in the back of his mind, where the beautiful girl he'd seen earlier had gone.

Abby

The girls who were hosting them that weekend were actually very sweet. Sure, they were serious about their studies and were homebodies of sorts, but Abby could see herself settling in with them next year, becoming just like them, and burying herself in her own studies as well.

She was going to teach. She'd never considered anything else as an option from the first summer she'd taught her own VBS class at her father's church. The kids that summer had been exhausting, energetic, and enlightening, all at the same time. She discovered that her love for Christ and her passion for His Word carried itself in her voice, in the way she shared, and in the way she made the abstract and theoretical real, even for first graders. Teaching was a gift, and Abby had that gift. Long after her father left ministry for good, wounded and weary, Abby found herself still drawn to opportunities to teach in the small church where she became a member on her own, where she nursed wounds dealt in ministry that even now still stung. She poured her passion and her belief that God was still good, despite the harm that His people had done, into the teaching she did in third grade Sunday school, second grade AWANA, and even a fifth grade girls' discipleship group. The only confusion she had about her collective experiences in teaching was which age she liked the best.

She was picking the right career. And that was a wonderful feeling.

Grant was not experiencing such a wonderful feeling, though, as evidenced by the way he sat outside in the hallway, holding his head in his hands, as she made her way back down the hallway. He glanced up when she was only a few steps away from him.

"Hey, Abs," he said, grinning.

"Hey," she answered, kicking his shoe with her own. "Almost did it this time, didn't you?"

"So close," he said. "So close. And you'd think I'd feel better after puking like that, but... I still feel so full."

She nodded, looking up as people began making their way out of the room, laughing and congratulating Grant on a good effort as they went.

"Rachel still in there?," she asked him.

"Yeah," he groaned. "Taking care of Seth." He rolled his eyes. "Like he needs it, the big wuss."

"No guy is going to refuse the attentions of a pretty young thing," Abby smiled.

"Which is why I thought Rachel dragged you here," he said. "To give me your attention, and –"

"Shut up, Grant," she laughed.

There had been a time, a few years ago, when there had been interest there. She had moved to the new town, the new school, and the new life God had dealt to her after her father left ministry, and Rachel was one of the first people she connected with in the crowded lunchroom full of teenage strangers. In no time at all, they were best friends, and Abby found herself, fourteen and shy, over at Rachel's house as often as she was in her own house. Grant was seventeen and spent most of his time ignoring them.

Until that next summer, as he prepared to leave for college, no longer as concerned, it seemed, by what his high school friends, already scattered to their different post-high school destinations, would think if he pursued his kid sister's friend. There were a few dates after a backyard BBQ where Abby and Grant found themselves alone in the kitchen, laughing and talking. He had uncovered one last dessert that evening, taking a bite for himself, smiling even as Abby watched him, then raising a bite to her lips as well. Very smooth for a seventeen year old boy, though at the time, Abby would have appreciated much less, believing as she did that Grant was the world.

It was strawberry shortcake, and she had only been able to relish the bite she had finished for a brief moment before Grant leaned over and gave her the first of many strawberry kisses he would give to her that summer.

There wasn't much there besides a lot of very sweet kisses. But she'd mourned his departure to college all the same, though not as much as Rachel had, especially when she met Seth, put two and two together, and proclaimed that the four of them could all get together and spend the rest of their lives together on one perpetual, neverending double date.

Yeah. After watching Grant throw up all of that milk, there would be no double dates anytime soon. Abby couldn't see him as anything but Rachel's very silly older brother and a very sweet, strawberry-flavored memory from younger days.

"You know what?," Grant said, looking up at her from where he continued sitting.

"What?"

"You should totally let me give you the grand tour of all the hot spots in the neighborhood," he said, "once you get here in the fall."

She looked at him doubtfully. "Hot spots in this neighborhood? Looks like the ghetto to me," she said.

"It is," he said. "Which means that maybe I should take you out farther than this neighborhood to the city, huh?"

"Rachel's always up for that," Abby said. "She probably knows more than you do anyway."

"I'm not going to take Rachel," he said. "I meant us – you and me."

She looked at him critically. "I think the milk's gone to your head, Grant."

He laughed out loud. "What?"

"That sounded like you were asking me out."

"Well, yeah," he said. "I mean, I've been thinking about it, and –"

And before he could finish his thought, the door to the room opened up again, and out stepped Seth's brother, a cell phone to his ear. Abby immediately stood taller, Grant all but forgotten as Stuart made his way towards them.

He glanced at her before looking back to Grant, saying goodbye to the person on the other end of the phone... then glancing back at her again.

"Hey, Stu," Grant said, clutching his stomach with no small amount of discomfort on his face. "Seth stop puking yet?"

Stuart's eyes flitted away from where they'd rested on Abby. "I think he's still got a couple of explosions left before it's all gone."

"Then I beat him after all," Grant grinned. "I only managed one. *One.*"

Abby rolled her eyes at this, prompting a small smile from the handsome stranger. She looked to Grant for an introduction.

"Oh, hey, Abs, this is Stu, Seth's brother," he said. "And Stu, this is Abs, and –"

He stopped abruptly, putting his hand to his mouth, jumping to his feet, and running to his room where they could already hear Rachel letting out a scream.

"He's probably not going to win," Stu murmured. He looked at her. "I'm guessing your name isn't really Abs."

"No," she said. "It's Abby... and you're probably a Stuart."

"Yeah," he nodded... then frowned at her. "Are you Grant's girlfriend?"

"No," she said, quickly. Because she so totally wasn't, even though Grant had been acting kind of funny, and –

Stu regarded her carefully. "Are you sure?"

"Yes, I'm sure," she said.

"Because he's been watching you all night and everything."

Abby considered this for a moment. "Really?"

He nodded.

"That's the strangest thing," she murmured. "I mean, we're not together. Geez, haven't been together in years. But he did just kinda ask me out, and that was pretty random, and –"

Hold the phones, Abby. Why was she telling him any of this?

"No," she said simply and succinctly, clearing her throat slightly as she did so, mortified that she had told this man so much unnecessary information. Maybe watching them drink all that milk had gone to *her* head.

"Dated him a long time ago, you say?," Stu asked, still interested in the topic.

"Yeah," she sighed. Might as well tell it all now, right? "Four years ago, actually."

He said nothing for a moment. "Well, then," he said, "where exactly did he take you on dates? Chuck E Cheese?"

"Excuse me?," she asked, not getting what he meant.

"Weren't you a little young four years ago? Obviously, since you're still very young –"

"I'm not that young," she said defensively. "I'll be done with high school in just a few weeks."

He practically scowled at this. "You're in high school?! What are you doing here, hanging out in a college guy's room all night?"

She didn't much like what he was saying... and what he wasn't saying. "I'm not staying in his room. And just who are you? My big brother? I'm here with Rachel, and –"

"Oh, man, *her*?"

"Well, yeah," Abby said. "What's wrong with Rachel?"

"Well," Stu sighed, "she's been trying her best to take advantage of poor, stupid Seth in there for the past three years now. That's the only reason I came back tonight, because I knew she'd be here, throwing herself at him. Knew he needed me here to help him keep his eyes on Christ and not on... well, you know."

There were several parts on Rachel that could serve as ample distractions for any normal man, especially one with a milk hangover. Abby could fill in the blanks. Which is probably why she was sufficiently offended on her friend's behalf.

"Seriously?," she asked him.

"Seriously," he said. "Gotta keep my kid brother on the straight and narrow. And Grant, too, likely with the way he's been watching you tonight."

As if *she* was someone who would have her way with Grant! As if Rachel was someone who would –

Okay, so she totally would have her way with Seth if he'd stop slipping through her clutches.

Even still, though.

Abby stepped up closer to him. "Look here, Stuart."

"Stu's fine."

"Stu, then," she hissed, pointing her finger at him. "I don't appreciate what you're saying about me."

"Haven't said anything about you," he said. "Just that Grant's been watching you like –"

"Yeah, I know," she sputtered. "Whatever. I don't know who you think you are, making all the assumptions you're making, but I'm a *good* girl, with high standards, and a walk with Jesus that you wouldn't know *anything* about, and –"

"And your skirt is way too short for a girl who's claiming all those things," he said.

"Excuse me?" Who was this bizarre man?

"Just telling it like I see it," he said. "Abby, right?"

"Yes," she said.

"I see it a lot," he said. "Freshmen come here, saying one thing about standards in all areas of their lives – academically, morally, ethically. And then? They chunk it all down the toilet after orientation. And I don't know what it is. Is it freedom from home? A lack of inhibitions?

Total insanity?" He shrugged. "I only mention it because, frankly? I'd love to mention it to every freshman who comes through here. So, I'm sharing my hard-earned wisdom with you."

While all he said was true enough, likely… well, it was weird that he had said any of it. To a stranger, nonetheless.

"That's about the most presumptuous thing I've ever heard," Abby muttered.

"You think?," he asked, raising his eyebrows. "You're here with that girl, Grant's looking at you like that, and that skirt you're wearing –"

"Yes," she huffed. "You've already mentioned that."

"Yeah, well, you didn't let me finish by saying that it works well with that completely inappropriate shirt that you're also wearing," he continued on. "Yeah, it's taking all that I have in me to keep looking you in the eyes right now."

She gasped out loud at this. How. *Dare*. He.

(Yeah, maybe the skirt was short. And maybe the shirt was tight. But unlike Rachel, she wasn't really flaunting anything, and it… well, it… darn him!)

Something in his eyes softened slightly. "I don't mean to be all… judgmental and all."

"Well, that's exactly what you're being," she answered him.

"I just see a beautiful young woman like you, who, by your own admission, loves Christ and wants to honor Him… and I feel compelled to step up and try to at least warn you about all that could happen here," he said. "You know. With an idiot like Grant. Or Seth either one. Because they're both idiots."

Well, Abby could agree to that.

And beautiful... well, that was... nice.

Kind of.

He watched her as she watched him, thinking on what an odd man he was. Well-spoken, of course, and persuasive but –

Before she could put her finger on what she really thought of him, Grant came back out into the hallway.

"Abs," he asked weakly, "do you think you could drive me to the ER?"

And while she doubted very much that Grant needed any medical intervention apart from a good swift kick in the butt for being an idiot, she welcomed the opportunity to get away from Stuart.

"Sure," she said. "Let's go."

And she walked away, not even bothering to look back.

Stu

He watched the girl walk away.

Abby.

Beautiful name. Beautiful girl. Beautiful words, about loving Christ.

He probably shouldn't have said half of what he had. Better now than during freshman orientation, when she'd find herself at some party with Rachel, and he'd be forced to kill some idiot guy who had her cornered, talking her into abandoning all of her convictions.

Or maybe she wouldn't be there. It was more likely that she'd be with Rachel, who would be with Seth, who, for all of his idiocy, was still a God-fearing idiot who kept the hijinks to a sedate gallon challenge now and then.

She'd be here. And he'd see her again.

"Where did Grant go?," Rachel asked him, coming out into the hall. "Are he and Abby…???" She looked up at Stu with wide, hopeful eyes.

"Are they what?," he asked.

"You know," she said. "*Together.* He asked me to make sure she came with me this weekend and –"

"No," Stu frowned. "I don't think she's into him like that."

"Probably not," Rachel sighed. "Though Grant would go for it. Maybe she'll change her mind."

Stu hoped she wouldn't. "No, she's taking him to the ER."

"The ER?," Rachel gasped. "What happened?"

Loud laughter from the doorway drifted over to them, and they turned to see Seth, leaning weakly on the doorframe and grinning.

"Bad, bad stuff," he chortled out. "There was the milk… and I slipped Grant a laxative earlier this evening."

Idiots.

"Seth," Rachel giggled, batting her eyelashes at him and sticking her chest out farther as she sauntered over to him. "You're so funny."

Funny and clueless as he continued to laugh, not even looking at her, even as she put her hand to his chest, curved into him –

"You're so stupid, man," Stu said, meaning many things with his statement.

"I know," Seth agreed. "But he had it coming. And now… well, something else will be coming his way shortly."

"Well, let's hope he makes it to the ER before it –" Rachel gasped. "Oh, crap!"

"Exactly," Seth burst out laughing all over again.

"No, Seth!," she shrieked. "Grant has *my* keys! He's going to poo all over my car!"

"And with your friend there," Stu said. Well, good. That would cure Abby of any Grant fascination she might still have. "How embarrassing."

"I've got to catch them!," she yelled, running down the hall in her tiny little skirt, strappy heels, and…

Seth wasn't even watching.

"You're an idiot," Stu said, for the hundredth time that night, likely.

"Oh, just good clean fun… if Rachel gets there in time." He smiled at his brother.

"No, I'm talking about Rachel."

"What about her?"

"Seth," he said, "you watch out for her. One day, she's going to get you alone and talk you into plenty before you ever even figure out that she has a mind to –"

"Nah," he said. "It's not like that. She's a kid."

"She's no kid," Stu argued. "And she's been watching you for years."

"Well, I don't see it," he sighed. "And I don't even think of her like that. You know that."

Stu nodded at this. "Be careful."

"I should tell you the same," he said, smiling. "I saw the way you were watching her friend."

Stu looked over to him. "You know anything about her?"

"Grant likes her," he said. "But I don't think she likes him. Seems nice enough, though. Was asking me about churches around here earlier. Already thinking ahead to the fall and figuring out where she'll end up."

"Sounds like she's got her priorities right," Stu murmured. "Did you tell her about our church?"

"Yeah," Seth smiled. "Of course." Then, he began laughing again.

"What?," Stu frowned.

"You like her," he said. "You really, really like –"

And with that, he turned back around, his hand to his mouth, and ran for the bathroom.

And Stu looked back down the hallway, hoping he'd see Abby again.

CHAPTER TWO

Abby

It had been a crazy, busy day. On top of a crazy, busy semester. And...
well, a crazy, busy college career.

She'd just finished up the last final of the fall semester and rejoiced that
with it, she was officially done with classes. One semester was all that
she now had left at the university, and it would all be practical, on-the-
field work, full of student teaching, at the school where she knew she'd
have a job in the fall if she wanted it. She was graduating a year early
because she'd had a plan from the very beginning and because she was
willing to endure more than one eighteen hour semester.

She sighed with a smile as she rushed into the dorm. The stress was
winding down, and she could put her attention to better pursuits and all
the wonderful things going on in her personal life, the hopes she had for
the plans she might soon be making for a future with him, and –

She jumped into the crowded elevator right before the doors could
close and glanced at the man who had put his hand out to stop them
from refusing her entry.

Stuart. *That* Stuart.

She made a big production of turning her back to him… and then spoke to him anyway.

"Long time no see, Stuart. Visiting your brother?," she asked, staring straight ahead.

"Nope," he sighed. "My brother graduated a long time ago. Thought you were dating his roommate and would've figured that out."

"I wasn't dating Grant," she muttered. "Thought we cleared that up."

"You did date him, though –"

"And your brother's gone, you say?," she interrupted him. "Must be why there hasn't been a gallon challenge in this dorm in years."

"I'm sure the cleaning staff is appreciative."

"Hmm," she murmured, fighting back a smile. "Where did your brother end up?"

"Vet school."

"That stinks. Literally, probably."

Silence. Neither one of them looked at one another as the elevator stopped, and one of the other students stepped out.

"So," she said, as the doors closed again. "What are you doing here if your brother is long gone?"

"Visiting my girlfriend," he said.

"Girlfriend," she murmured. "Still stuck here at college, dating underclassmen –"

"Well, she's in her third year," he said. "Crazy smart, because she's only twenty-one and only a semester away from graduation."

Abby sighed. "She sounds boring."

One of the other students glanced over at her uncomfortably. She shrugged in response.

"Well, she's anything but boring," Stuart murmured. "Smart, of course. Passionate about her studies. Already pursuing a career. So incredibly godly. And beautiful."

"Wow," Abby scoffed. "Why is she with you, Stuart?"

"Because I talked her into the idea," he replied confidently. "She couldn't resist."

"I'll bet."

"Or maybe I should say that she took pity on me. Poor, sad, lonely Stuart. So in need of a little love, care, and attention. Is that better?"

Abby grinned. "So, she's compassionate, too?"

"Extremely so."

"And she's twenty-one, you say?" Abby whistled. "My, my... that's young."

"I know," he said. "But not as young now as when I first took her out. She was only nineteen back then."

"Did you take her to Chuck E Cheese?," Abby asked.

"No," he said, and she could hear the grin in his voice. "Though that would have been fun."

More silence as another student stepped off the elevator. Only three remained. Stuart, Abby, and a guy who kept checking his phone.

"Big plans for tonight, huh?," she asked. "Based on the way you're dressed."

"Well, yes, to the big plans. But, no, this is how I dress every day."

"Big job in the corporate world, huh?"

"Yeah," he said. "Working in a political party office. And frankly, it sucks most days."

She bit her lip, thinking on this. "Picked the wrong career?"

"Most days I think so," he murmured. "Thought I'd be changing the world. All I'm doing is talking up people, raising money."

"Something tells me that you're good at that, though," she said. "Charming people and getting them to open their wallets."

"Like any good politician, I guess," he said. "Oh, well. It's just a job. And it pays the bills. And I plan on charging up a big bill tonight for the celebratory dinner."

"What are you celebrating?," she asked.

"My girl's birthday," he said, "and two years together."

"Smart of you to do that," she said. "Combining big events like that. You can get by with one gift."

"Yeah," he laughed. "And the gift tonight? Beyond amazing."

"You should tell me what it is," she said, smiling, still not looking over at him. "I can tell you whether or not she'll like it, I'll bet."

Another pause, as the elevator opened, and the last remaining student stepped off. Abby watched him go, while Stu stepped up to the panel, pressed the button to close the doors, and waited until the elevator began to climb again. Then, he turned to her with a slow smile, stepped up close to her and put his hands to her face. "You're not getting your gift early, Abby."

"Come here," she grinned, pulling him close and putting her lips to his. Then, after an intoxicating few moments, she sighed. "That alone is better than whatever you're planning on giving me later."

"Oh, I know." He went right back to kissing her, without hardly taking a breath. "I appreciate how you pretend you don't know me like that every now and then."

"I pretend that you're a stranger," she said, closing her eyes as he continued kissing her face, "and see if you can win me over all over again. And you do, Stu. Every single time."

"Mmmhmm..."

"There are only, like, three floors left," she said, poking him in the chest. "You're getting things started, and you –"

"What am I getting started?," he asked around her lips, not even bothering to stop his slow, meticulous kisses. He moved to just below her ear, kissing oh so slowly, and murmuring, "Tell me, Abby..."

Oh, geez. "Stu..."

"Just asking," he murmured, the smile evident in his voice as he put his lips to her neck, ran his hands down her back and to her waist.

"You know good and well what you're doing," she sighed, pulling his face up to meet hers and very nearly wrapping herself around him. "Just like those idiot boys you warned me about before I even started classes here."

"Yes, and I'm praising the Lord that you put some modesty back in your wardrobe because it's hard enough to concentrate on anything but you as it is, dressed like you are, and I can't imagine what –"

The elevator stopped.

"And," he whispered, planting one long, last kiss to her lips, then stepping back gallantly, "now I get to walk you to your room and wait out in the hallway like the perfect gentleman that I am."

She put her hand to her mouth, her heart racing as he took her hand in his and strode off the elevator with her following him.

"Too smooth for your own good," she said softly. "Or maybe it's my own good."

He gave her a slow smile. "Smooth enough that I talked you into going out with me two years ago, didn't I?"

He had. He really had. She had gone home after Preview Weekend, certain she'd never see him or hear from him again. And no loss there since she had absolutely no interest in him. She'd finished high school, worked through the summer, and came back in the fall, ready for all the classes that would make her dreams a reality.

Part of that freshman load included an Introduction to Political Science class. She'd only have three hours of Poli Sci, and she was certain that it couldn't pass quickly enough, since she had absolutely no interest in the subject. The day she arrived in the huge lecture hall, she was surprised to find that the class was being team-taught by a group of graduate students, hand-selected by the university.

And she was slightly mortified that the graduate student assigned to her was the very same Stuart Huntington that she had told off the spring before.

He had recognized her instantly, raising his eyebrows at her slightly as he gave her a stack of handouts to pass down the front row she sat on, right before he began lecturing the entire thousand-student room. She kept her eyes averted the whole time, concentrating on her notes.

The semester had gone on… more pleasantly than she thought it would. The huge class felt increasingly smaller when she was picked to lead a study group based on her test scores and the papers she wrote, and she found herself looking forward to the sessions after hours, when Stuart would be there, assisting and teaching as the study group leaders met together… and then after, as the rest would leave and she'd be left talking with him. When she found a church in the college town, she was only slightly less mortified to see that it was Stuart's church as well. But before long, the best part of her week was the hour she spent at the young adult Bible study he taught there, always asking her opinion, always smiling when she told him what she thought.

He was conservative. And he spoke his mind. The preview she'd gotten of him at, fittingly enough, Preview Weekend was an accurate one. Stuart knew who he was, knew how people were, and knew how to express himself. Hours of conversation together, moments and snippets of time shared throughout those few months, drew a different picture of him in her mind. And she respected him as an intelligent, ambitious man, admired who he was in Christ, and valued his… friendship.

Because it was friendship, even if she caught herself wondering what it would be like if she reached out, grabbed him, and whispered, "Come here," before laying her lips on his.

Friendship.

She went to his office right before Christmas to contest the B she knew was coming her way, based on the way he'd graded her last paper. It would keep her off the dean's list, and she wasn't having it, especially not with all the extra work she'd done with the study group.

"Abby," he said, lightly tossing the paper to his desk as she sat across from him, her backpack in her lap. "You're right when you say you deserve an A for your work in the class."

"Thank you," she said. "So, this paper is –"

"This paper is a complete anomaly," he said. "It's sub-par compared to your other work. But still, giving you an A, after this paper, wouldn't be fair."

She said nothing for a minute. "All my other work, then? Doesn't matter?"

"I graded you by the same standard as everyone else," he said calmly.

"You graded me *harder* than you graded them," she said. And it was true. He held her to a different standard, almost as if to compensate for the way they shared looks, spoke to one another... seemed to feel.

"Because you're smarter," he said simply. "And because that's just the way it is. Not like making a B is a bad thing, you know."

She had frowned at him. "Fine, then. My first B. Ever. Thank you so much."

"You'll be a stronger person for it, Abby," he said, smiling.

"I'm starting to rethink the wisdom of signing up for your stupid section next semester," she spat out. So, she'd opted for another semester of Poli Sci. She liked the subject, she liked the time spent in study... she liked the teacher.

He raised his eyebrows at this. "I don't want you to take my section," he said. "In fact, I'm going to remove you from it myself and put you in someone else's."

Before she could respond to the way this stung, he leaned forward on his desk.

"I want things to be different next semester," he said.

"Me, too," she managed. "I'd like to get an A in *all* of my classes, and actually make–"

"Nope," he said. "Me. You. Different."

She watched him for a moment. "I don't know what you mean."

"Yes, you do," he smiled. "You know it as well as I do."

"Are you asking me out?," she whispered, aware that they could probably be heard by other faculty members.

"I think we're well beyond that, Abby," he murmured.

And she thought of all of the genuine, true moments between them, how he wasn't like any other guy she'd ever known. This would be different. This would be serious. This would be a forever and ever kind of deal once it started.

Because Stuart was a forever and ever kind of guy.

"But, no," he said, "I'm not 'asking you out' because you're my student for the next…" He looked at the calendar on his wall. "One week, two days, and three hours. That's when grades are due, and you'll no longer be my student."

She grinned at this… and okay, so she blushed a little. "Keeping close tabs on that, huh, Stu?"

"You have no idea," he sighed. "Well, actually, you probably have some idea. If how you've been looking at me is any indication."

She narrowed her eyes at this. Then smiled again. "Well, probably."

And understanding passed between them as they looked at one another, as it had on more than one occasion over the semester. Abby felt quite warm and gooey at the very thought of all those moments…

He gave her a smile in return. "Then one week, two days, and three hours…"

But it didn't take that long.

In fact, that very night, he showed up at the girls' dorm with a Thermos full of hot chocolate. He wasn't allowed upstairs to the common areas after hours, but instead of shouting up to her window like the boys who had girlfriends in the building, he came into the lobby, chatted with the dorm security officer, and called her on the phone in the front hall.

"Abby," he said, in an exaggerated gallant tone that she knew must have been partially for the amusement of the guards and yet still completely for her alone, "I was wondering if perhaps you would like to take a walk across campus with me?"

She was down the stairs and by his side literally one minute after hanging up the phone, prompting a huge smile from him. "Here is your beverage of choice," he told her, holding out the hot chocolate, touching her fingers for longer than absolutely necessary as she took it from him.

"You picked up on that during all those nights in the study group, huh?"

"Accidentally picked up your cup and took a drink one night while you were in the ladies' room," he said. "Thought you were a coffee drinker… but you were just a poser, drinking hot chocolate like it was the strong stuff."

"I'm a total poser, and I hate coffee," she whispered. "But I love this. Thanks, Stu."

He watched her for a moment, wordless as she smiled at him. "What?," she asked, feeling a whole litany of wonderful, sweet, overwhelming, incredible emotions in the warmth of his gaze –

"Just thinking," he whispered, smiling.

Minutes later, they were walking side by side, talking through finals, through all the studying and grading, and about what their plans were for the weeks ahead.

"I just want the semester to be over with already," she told him, thinking about the break, about the draining study… about that one week, two days, and three hours.

"Ready to go home, huh?," he asked.

"Yeah," she said. "Though… I'll miss seeing you."

Without a word, he reached out and took her hand. "Me, too." A pause. "Maybe I can come visit you."

"Yeah," she managed, inexplicably shy at the admission in his suggestion, in the hand that held hers. "I'd love that."

"Then, we'll make it happen," he said, pulling her even closer.

"Hey," she nudged him with her shoulder. "We've still got the one week, two –"

"Yeah, about that," he said, stopping and turning to her. "I finished up my grades this afternoon, right after we finished talking."

"Really?"

"Yeah, you're getting a B," he said.

She didn't much care at this point, actually. "You did them early?"

"I spent the whole afternoon and all evening, up until ten minutes ago, finishing those grades," he said. "I'm no longer, in any way, shape, or form, in any position of authority over you at this fine, fine institution."

"Well," she sighed, "that's wonderful news. Not about the B, of course, but –"

"But," he whispered, reaching out and touching her face tenderly. "About us."

"Yeah," she managed, thinking that his hands were magic as he continued stroking her cheek. "That's... great and all."

All around them were students, coming and going from class to the library to the cafeteria to the student center, laughing and celebrating the end of the semester, cramming for one last final, talking about all that was left to do, making so much noise... and she couldn't hear or see any of them as she stared at Stuart, as Stuart stared at her.

Before she could even take a breath – actually, make that start breathing again – he put both hands on her face, tilted it just so, and put his lips on hers. Right there under the light, in the only cold of the season, a warm Thermos of hot chocolate in her hand.

And she had the fleeting thought, even as he kissed her, that this would be the last first kiss she'd ever have, that she'd never want anyone the way she wanted Stuart Huntington, and that life would never, ever be the same.

Thrilling. Terrifying. World-changing. Wonderful.

Even still.

Abby smiled to think on the memory, even now as he led her down the hallway, glancing over his shoulder at her, wondering at the look on her face.

"What?," he asked softly.

"Just thinking," she answered him.

"About your gift," he nodded. "I know how you are."

She laughed at the smirk he gave to her. "I'm just glad you're not going to make it into my Christmas gift as well," she said. "That's the worst thing about a December birthday. People are always trying to stiff you on presents."

"There will still be a present at Christmas," he nodded. "You just have to endure the holiday with my family in order to get it. Or, you know, the pseudo-holiday before the actual holiday since we couldn't get everyone together on Christmas Day."

"That's what you get with a gigantic family," she smiled. She'd met the whole horde of Huntingtons a handful of times, but this would be her first major holiday with them. The thought left her... a little nervous.

"Sam's going to be home," Stu said. "Back from Afghanistan for a while."

"All six of you under one roof, finally," she said. "I'll bet your mother is beside herself."

"All six of us. And you. Oh, and Jennie."

"Great company there, with Jennie and all," Abby sighed. "What's she doing now? Writing books on how to be the perfect wife while simultaneously feeding all the starving children in Africa?"

So, she felt a little… inadequate, up next to Jennie. Sean, Stuart's oldest brother, had married the perfect woman. Thin, beautiful, outgoing, and accomplished – she was ministry-bound and focused before she even met Sean. They'd married, combining their talents and goals into a ministry machine, and planted a church together, which had since sprung another campus. Sean was a trendy, edgy pastor reaching a millennial generation, and Jennie was his hip, fashionable, and authentic ministry wife.

Except her authenticity reflected her perfection and left everyone else feeling very small. Or at least she made Abby feel that way. None of Stu's other brothers had wives or serious girlfriends, so every time they got together, it was just her and Jennie trying to mesh into the mess.

Jennie was managing to do so artfully. Abby… well, Abby wasn't.

Stu watched her, smiling. "She's not perfect. And she's only written the one book, you know."

"Just one book," Abby murmured. "*Only* one book."

"And," he said, laughing, stopping just outside her door, pulling her into his arms, "she didn't feed any starving children in Africa. She was on a water purification team."

"Even better," Abby laughed. "You'd think she and I would have a world of things in common, but I think it's just Jesus… and Huntington men. And that's it."

"Jesus and Huntington men," he said, reaching for the doorknob, "what a –"

He threw his hand up to his eyes, just as Rachel shrieked at him.

"Geez, Stu! It's called *knocking*!" She stood there in jeans and a bra, clutching her T shirt to her chest. "Did you *see* anything?!"

"Nope," he said. "Just enough to see that you were in the room."

"And you covered your eyes at that?," she asked, clearly not believing him, pulling her shirt on over her head.

"Better safe than sorry."

"Well, I'm covered up now," she said.

Abby smiled over at her, while pulling Stu's hands from his eyes. "He's a good guy, Rachel. Isn't he?"

"Yeah, I guess," Rachel sighed. "What was he saying about Jesus and Huntington men? Are you talking about Seth?"

"No," he said, "I wasn't talking about Seth."

"How is he?," Rachel asked. "I haven't gotten down there to see him in a while."

Rachel wasn't dating Seth. Rachel had never dated Seth. This didn't mean that Rachel didn't make trips to visit him, didn't send care packages to him, didn't call him randomly... didn't practically already have her name written right into the Huntington family Bible.

As much as Abby loved Stu, even she wasn't half as serious about becoming Mrs. Huntington as Rachel was.

"He's doing good," Stu answered, patiently. "Taking a few days off for the holidays, at least."

"Tell him I'll be by soon with his Christmas present," she smiled. "And maybe I'll stop by and visit with your mom, too, Stu. Sure have missed chatting with her."

See? Name very nearly in the family Bible.

"Abs," she went on, missing Stu's raised eyebrows, "are you going out tonight? There's a group going to look at Christmas lights if you want to come with us."

"I've just been informed," Abby said, wrapping her arms around Stu, "that I have big plans."

Rachel sighed just slightly, as Stu kissed her friend. "Well, that figures."

"Yeah," Stu said. "And I'm going to go outside to the TV lounge and wait while you get ready."

"I'm going to wear that dark green dress I bought a few weeks ago," she said to him, straightening his tie as she did so. "Sound good?"

"I love that dress," he smiled. "And I love you."

"Me, too, Stu."

"Gag, gag, gag," Rachel murmured, rolling her eyes, then grinning at Stu. "Big plans tonight, you say?"

"Yeah," he said, his eyes never leaving Abby. "Better leave soon. I'll be waiting for you, okay?" And with a quick kiss goodbye, he was out, and Abby was shutting the door behind him, facing her friend with a sly grin and fanning herself off dramatically.

"The two of you are nauseating," Rachel said, very simply.

"Well, I am feeling all fluttery inside, that's for sure," Abby laughed.

"That man is going to propose tonight, Abby," Rachel proclaimed.

And though Abby had thought about marriage more than a few times, this was still thrilling, surprising, and... well, too good to be true.

"He is not," she said, beginning to undress.

"Please," Rachel sighed. "Apart from the way he was looking at you, the way he's *always* looking at you, there's the whole 'big plans' thing. And it's your birthday. And your anniversary. Big gift, right?"

"He may have said that," Abby nodded, pulling at her shoes. Then, glancing up at Rachel, "But I still have one more semester to go. And I'm not even sure where I'll end up, where I'll find a job, after it's all said and done."

"What better time than now, then?," Rachel asked. "You say yes tonight, spend all semester getting yourself prepared to be in the same place, and marry him this summer. It's worked out rather perfectly, don't you think?"

And it would be perfect. Even still, though, surely it wouldn't... he wouldn't...

Well, he could. And two years of dating? Was more than enough time for a man as bold and brash as Stu usually was, saying what he thought all the time, to make such a huge decision.

It was more surprising that he had taken so long, actually.

"You really think he's going to ask me to marry him?," Abby asked, smiling.

"Oh, yeah," Rachel said. "And I swear, Abs, you better pair me up with Seth for the wedding. I'm talking hosting a coed shower with him, walking down the aisle with him, sitting by him at the reception... even making the groomsmen do a first dance with the bridesmaids. You can make that happen, right?"

And Abby, who was sure that all of her dreams were about to come true, was convinced that she could make anything happen.

"You bet, Rachel."

Stu

It was going to be a big night. A huge night.

The ring was in his pocket already, and he knew just when he'd get down on one knee, say all the things he'd said before, and ask her to go where God led them together.

Of all the things that would appeal most to Abby in his proposal, Stu knew that it would be the desire to go where God wanted to lead them. It was what he loved most about her and was the very thing that had changed his interest from a curiosity over the sassy girl who came to Preview Weekend to a great attraction for the bright, young woman who sat front row, center at the Bible study class he led at church.

She'd tried her best to avoid him after that first Poli Sci class, never even making eye contact with him as he lectured, not even as he tried to approach her afterwards, as she slipped into the crowds and hustled out. He half expected to see her drop the class that first week, but her name was still on his roster going into the weekend. She was going to stick it out and ignore him, likely.

However, that would be difficult to do since God apparently had other plans, putting them into the same situation that Sunday morning at church.

It was a smaller situation, obviously, with only fifty young adults there in the class. Abby looked plenty mortified as he sat down and made a general welcome to the newcomers, looking to her for a second longer than he would have normally.

Stu was convinced that she wouldn't have said a word had he been teaching any other book of the Bible that fall. But as it was, he was in the middle of Romans, and as he soon discerned, not even five minutes into class, Abby's theology was not nearly as reformed as his.

He asked questions of the entire class. Abby answered most of them. He gave her other Scriptures as he debated her stance. She gave him more Scripture. He told her the Greek. She told him he was doing a poor job of parsing the Greek. Their debate became so animated that the entire class was pulled in, over only half of one verse.

It was the best discussion he'd ever had in his class.

When it came time for the worship service, Stu reached out a hand and touched her arm, freezing her in place while the rest of the students left the room.

"Abby," he said, remembering her name, of course.

"Stuart," she sighed... remembering his, too.

"Welcome to First Community Church," he said.

"Thanks," she frowned. "Though I'm not sure I'll be back."

"Didn't enjoy Sunday school, huh?"

She sighed. "Enjoyed it plenty, but... this is probably not the class for me."

He grinned. "Probably not, since your comprehension is leaps and bounds above everyone else's."

"I figured that," she said, "when no one came out and quoted Scripture telling me that women are to remain silent in the church."

"They probably didn't even realize that's *in* Scripture, honestly."

"And I'm glad for it," she said, "as I find myself in a situation where I can't exactly go home and ask questions of or be taught by a father or husband either one, as Scripture would suggest I do."

"So instead," Stu smiled, "you ask me. And by asking me, I mean you tell me, in front of the entire class, that I've got it all wrong."

She frowned. "You should have sent me on to a different class."

"Never even crossed my mind," he said, smiling even more broadly, "even when you told them all that I had... what was it? A poor comprehension of the text, along with an alarming linguistic deficiency?"

She blushed. "Still managed to sound like you knew what you were talking about, though. Even if you didn't."

"Yeah, thanks for that," he said. "How do you know any of this?"

"I study," she said. "When something's important to you, you study it."

"Obviously," he said. "I can appreciate someone who studies Scripture like that. And I can appreciate that someone even more when she brings life to an otherwise quiet, dull class."

She bit her lip. "Well, it was a good class. You... well, you did your best. Made me think, at least."

He grinned. "You should come back every week."

"Well," she said, "this is the first church I've visited. I mean, I don't know where I'll end up —"

"End up here," he said. "You could spend the rest of your college years floating from church to church. This is a good place, with good people, sound doctrine. Plant yourself here."

And he wasn't all that surprised to see her join that same Sunday... and when she was back in Poli Sci the next week, she let her eyes meet his. Finally.

And he hadn't taken his eyes off of her since.

He said what he thought, all the time, but he had censored his words that first fall. She was his student, and he knew the boundaries. But he relished every moment spent with her, looked for more opportunities to hear her speak her mind, and found himself trading smiles and looks and wondering glances with her as they neared the end of the semester.

The grades that semester were the quickest he had ever computed and submitted, so ready to be done with his position and the unavailable position he was in when it came to her. He'd been fearful most of the semester that someone else would ask her out, that she'd take them up on their offer, and that he'd lose his chance before he even got a chance.

But she hadn't seemed to be interested in anyone. She was much more interested in the book of Romans and Poli Sci... and maybe more, he thought, as she smiled at him over her backpack, even as he told her she wouldn't be on the dean's list after all.

It had been two years since that night under the lightpost on campus, and the bold, brash "I love you" that had followed mere weeks later was true even now. It would always be true.

He put his hand in his pocket, even as he glanced at the clock, wondering when she'd be ready, and felt the ring box again.

"Hey," he heard her whisper in his ear, just as she slipped her arms around him from behind. "You ready to go?"

He turned to her slowly, smiled, and took a breath. "Yeah. I'm ready."

Abby

She knew as he drove, one hand on the wheel, the other in her lap where she held it in hers, that this could be it.

Even though Stu had been part of every future plan she'd made these last two years, she was still nervous. Not about him, not about what would be, but about the huge moment before them.

"You okay?," he asked softly, looking over at her.

"Yeah," she nodded, smiling. "Just... busy day. Busy semester."

He raised her hands to his lips and kissed them. "I've missed you this semester. Feels like we haven't been able to see each other as often."

And it was true. Stu had finished up his degree in the spring and had jumped headlong into the job with the political party, doing what he thought would be analysis work and platform-building. As it turned out, though, the job was more about raising money and schmoozing rich people than anything else. Abby well remembered the Saturday they'd spent at his apartment earlier on in the semester, talking over the disappointment from his work as they ate the meal she'd cooked for him.

"Real work sucks, huh?," Abby asked as Stu had picked at his plate from where he sat on the floor.

"Yeah," he sighed, looking up to where she sat on the couch. "It does indeed suck. You know, I went into this all thinking that I could change the world... and all I'm doing is acting as a pimp for the organization."

Abby coughed at this. "A pimp? It's not all that bad, surely."

"Well, maybe not that bad," he sighed. "But it's not what I planned on doing with my life. It feels... sleazy. Wrong, somehow. And I can talk my way through it and around it and all over it, but there's just no excitement or joy in it. Not like you and teaching."

No, it wasn't like her with the teaching. She volunteered at a local school, on top of her eighteen hour course load, because she so loved working with children. She knew already with the degree she was getting just what her job would look like, and she knew she'd walk into a situation that was everything she had expected.

Predictable. Secure. Safe.

Not unlike Stu himself, who even then had looked up at her admirably. "I want to like what I do," he said simply, "like you do."

"Maybe there's something worth liking in it, Stu," she said. "Think of what the dollars you earn for the party do to change the world. Maybe that's what God has for you right now. And it doesn't mean that it'll always be what He has for you."

He raised his eyebrows at this. "Maybe. It could be that God has something else entirely planned for me down the road, huh?"

She thought on this. "Well… in politics. In what you've already worked so hard to get to." She grinned. "Don't go joining the circus on me, Stu."

He grinned at this. "Scoot over," he said, moving from the floor and up next to her on the couch, sliding his arms around her as she took the bite on her fork and raised it to his lips, watching as he ate it.

"Mmm," he murmured, leaning down to brush his lips against hers. "Yours is even better than mine was."

"They're exactly the same," she sighed, returning his kiss.

"I like yours better."

"Figured you would," she said. "Split the rest with me."

"Is this how we're going to make do when I run off and join the circus? Splitting meals, cutting costs, making our way in the world by performing like little monkeys, and –"

"I'm sorry," she laughed, giving him a smile. "Who said I was running away with you? I don't even like the circus."

He grinned. "But you like me."

"I do like you, Stu."

"And I figure," he said softly, whispering it in her ear, "that wherever we go, we'll go together."

And she had closed her eyes at the very thought, inhaling his scent even as he kissed her cheek.

Wherever. Together.

Even now, even still, as they headed towards wherever it was that Stuart had arranged big plans, she smiled at the thought.

And she squeezed his hand again, so eager to make this a forever kind of deal.

Stu

He knew she knew the restaurant. He knew she'd know the significance of it.

Sure enough, as soon as they pulled up to the parking lot, she'd squeezed his hand, smiling.

He'd taken her there before, on the first really fancy date they'd gone on her freshman year, after an incredible holiday season where he'd spent hundreds of dollars on the tanks of gas it took to get to her, to sit talking with her for hours, to learn everything about her.

She'd been as serious about him as he was about her, even back then.

He'd known the truth of it on the night he told her, as they sat in her parents' living room, long after everyone else had gone to sleep, about who he'd been before Christ had changed his life in college.

It had been Seth's disappointment in him that had set the change in motion from an earthly perspective at least. It had been entirely Christ behind the change, though, as Stu began to question his purposes, his future, and his very identity, in the light of how very far he'd come from what he'd been raised to believe, what he thought he had believed all along.

He hadn't really believed, if the fruit in his life was any indication.

But that had changed. And he had mourned what he'd been in the meantime, the mistakes he had made. And he mourned it anew, in a fresh and painful way, as Abby struggled to keep her tears in check, no judgment in her eyes, as he shared it all with her.

"We all have a past," she said softly.

"Not you," he said, swallowing past the lump in his throat, even as he reached out and touched her cheek.

And she couldn't keep a tear from falling over his fingers. "No, but there are other things that… well, that are baggage for me. For us."

"I can't imagine what they'd be," he said. "Or fathom that they could be worse than what I've done. If I had known," he said very simply, "that God was bringing you to me, all those years ago, I would've done differently."

"It was against Christ, not me," she said. "And you've felt the pain of that, in grieving it though He redeemed it, and I won't make you feel grief over it all a second time." She said nothing for a moment. "That's the good Christian girl answer I'm supposed to give, right, Stu?"

He shrugged. "I don't know what the right answer is. I only know that I'm regretting things that much more, sitting here and telling you about it. Be honest with me. Does this change things?"

"No," she sighed, wiping away tears. "Not at all. It's just..." She bit her lip, holding back more tears.

"What?," he whispered. "Abby, tell me what you're thinking..."

She reached out to touch his face. "You're mine. And everything you had to give and gave back then... was mine. I'm just a little sad thinking about it. But I won't think about it ever again, Stu. And I won't bring it up again. Because it's over and done. And you're mine now."

And he'd held her for a long while that night, thinking through the simplicity and the profound truth, all at the same time, of redemption coming a second time through this forgiveness, being someone new in Christ, and being hers.

He was ready from that moment on to make this a forever kind of deal.

And back in the restaurant, as they celebrated two years together, he was going to follow through on it all.

Abby didn't know the direction of his thoughts as he looked across the table at her, desserts finished and done before them.

"Stu, you should have talked me out of the chocolate," she said. "I've eaten way too much. You'll have to roll me out of here."

He swallowed and shifted in his seat, feeling the weight of the ring in his pocket, reaching down to pull it out, as she watched him.

"Are you okay?," she asked, softly.

He took a deep breath, then looked her fully in the face. "You know how much I care about you, don't you?"

"Yeah," she managed, taking a deep breath herself. "I know."

And he got down on one knee, even as she gasped and said, "Stu, wait!"

This wasn't what he expected, clearly, as he blinked at her. "Is something wrong?"

"Oh, Stu," she said, "everything is absolutely perfect!"

"Okay," he said, holding the box awkwardly in his hand. "Then, should I…" He gestured. "Go ahead?"

She nodded, tears in her eyes. "Yeah, I just… wanted time. To remember it all. To make sure I don't forget how you looked, the music that was playing… everything. I just wanted time."

He grinned. "Are you saying you need more time?"

"No," she smiled, actually crying now. "I know for sure. My answer is yes."

"You know," he said with a smile, "most girls would want to see the ring before they made up their mind."

"I know," she laughed. "But the best part of this whole deal," she said, placing her hands on either side of his face, "is you, Stuart Huntington." She planted a kiss squarely on his lips, lingering there for a moment, holding his face to hers, until he wrapped his arms around her waist and leaned his forehead against hers.

"Do you want to marry me, Abby?," he asked, the ring box in his hands entirely forgotten.

"Stu," she murmured, kissing his lips. "I do. I do, I do, I do."

And for a moment, they both closed their eyes, oblivious to the applause of all the others in the restaurant.

CHAPTER THREE

Abby

Christmas at the Huntington house was different this year. Because by this time next year, she would be a Huntington herself.

Well, that was still a thrill, even a week into their engagement. She stole a glance down at her ring, which connected her eyes to Stu's hand, the hand that hadn't let go of hers since he'd picked her up that morning.

"You ready?," he asked, just outside the front door.

"It's not like I've never met them before," she said. "Well, with the exception of Sam."

"You've met them," he affirmed, "but now, you're *one of us*." He waved his fingers at her, making an odd face as he did so.

"Not quite yet," she said.

"Not soon enough," he murmured, leaning in to kiss her before he put his free hand to the doorknob, just as it opened up to them both…

And there he stood, a knowing smile on his face as he nodded her direction. "What's up, Abby." A statement rather than a question.

"Hey, Scott," she said. "Merry Christmas."

"Yeah," he sighed. "Ho, ho, ho and all that. Hey, Stu Man. You're looking... okay. But Abby here? Is looking *much* nicer than just okay. In fact, Abby, do you wanna leave my little brother here, go ahead and sneak off with me and skip the drama of –"

"Scott," Stu said, "are you already drinking?"

Scott put his hand to his chest dramatically, pretending to be offended. "Well, I may have had a... few. But hardly worth counting, Stuart, especially if you reason, as I do, that for every relative I have to deal with today, I deserve at least one drink." A pause. "One drink per relative, that is. And I'll drink them all on my own, of course."

"Everyone here already?," Stu asked, as Abby put her arms around his waist.

"Yep," he said. "All of the Huntingtons, at least. And now that you guys are here, the topic of conversation will be the wedding, instead of Sam." He grinned at Abby. "Come on, let me see it." He held his hand out for hers.

She smiled at him and slipped her left hand into his, letting him hold up the ring for his inspection. He whistled.

"Very nice," he said. "Of course, I have no idea what I'm even supposed to look for, but the women sure will." He looked Abby in the eyes as he kissed her hand. "I'd have probably said yes, too, if Stu had slipped this on my finger."

"I have better taste than that," Stu muttered, "and better sense."

"Let's hope so," he laughed, embracing Abby and pulling them both into the house, where they were met with instant shrieking as Stu's younger sister raced over to them.

"Let me see, let me see, let me see!," Savannah screeched, literally pushing Scott right out of her way. "STUUUUU...," she groaned, as she shot her brother a huge smile. "You did GREAT!" Then, shouting, "Hey, Jennie! Come here and check this out!" She winked at Abby, right before pulling her in for a hug, whispering in her ear, "Gonna hack Mrs. Perfect off, since Sean couldn't afford something this fabulous when he proposed to her."

Abby frowned at her sister-in-law to be, just as her other sister-in-law to be sauntered up, her perfect, plastic, pastor's wife smile in place.

"Hello, Abby!," she practically sang, tilting her head to the side. "Congratulations on the en-gage-ment!" Seriously, everything was singsong.

"Well, thank you," Abby said, fighting against the urge to sing it as well.

"Check out the rock, Jennie!," Savannah said, holding Abby's hand up in victory.

"Oh, my," Jennie breathed softly. "Stuart, that ring is simply beau-ti-ful." Then softly, "I do hope you made sure it was a conflict-free diamond, though."

"Conflict-free?," Abby asked, confused.

"Oh, yes," Jennie said, slightly gasping. "Children in Africa, slave labor, practically, all for these little stones. Blood diamonds, Abby. Horrible things all in the name of —"

"Giant rocks," Savannah finished, taking Abby's hand back so as to have another look. "That ain't no little stone that Stu bought."

"Well, no, it isn't," Jennie agreed, glancing at Abby's hand with concern.

"Conflict-free," Stu chimed in, sliding his arm around Abby's waist. "I remember the pictures you showed us from your trip, Jennie. I made sure these diamonds were from a better source. Even found one that does charitable work for those children. Cost much more than it should have, but... well, Abby's worth it."

"Gaaaaaaahhhh," Savannah groaned as Jennie gave him a smile. "You're my brother, and you're making me SWWOOOOONNNN, Stu Man!" She sighed. "You and Sam both. But the rest? I can just do without. Scott's a creepy alcoholic –"

"Takes one to know one," Scott shouted from the kitchen.

"Yeah, and Seth's a complete nerd, still in his books even though it's freakin' Christmas break, and Sean is acting like he's got a pole rammed right up his –"

"He has a lot on his plate with that new church plant," Jennie interrupted her, frowning. "And, Savannah, I –"

"Speaking of plates," the beautiful, blond woman coming out of the kitchen said, "we'll be ready to eat as soon as Emily and Josh get here." She stopped in front of Abby, reaching out to hug her. "Welcome to the family, Abby. I couldn't have asked for a better girl for my boy."

"Thanks, Mrs. Huntington," Abby managed, almost shyly, over her future mother-in-law's shoulder.

"It's Jess," she said. "No more formalities. You're family now, and –"

"If she's family, can I unbutton my pants at the dinner table?," Scott bellowed from the kitchen. "All these appetizers have got me –"

"Keep your pants on," another male voice boomed, as the stranger it belonged to came out of the kitchen and walked right up to Stu. The resemblance between them was startling, magnified by the matching smiles they wore as they saw one another.

"Sam," Stu said, reaching out to hug his brother. "It was worth coming home just to see you."

"Well, worth coming back to meet your fiancée, definitely," Sam answered, turning to Abby and reaching out to shake her hand. "Hey, Abby, I'm Sam."

"I think I could've figured that out," she said, holding his hand in hers for a moment. "You're like Stuart, version 2.0."

"It would be more accurate to call him Sam, version 2.0, since I'm older, but point taken," he said, reaching out and messing up Stu's hair. "The politician and the Marine. Kinda in the same business... in a weird sort of way."

"Not a politician," Stu laughed. "Just a minion and a chess piece for the real politicians."

"Funny that," Sam murmured back. "I kinda feel like that myself most days."

"Who cares about that," Savannah said, pulling him towards the kitchen. "You're on leave. For three blissful weeks. We'll get you for *three* weeks!"

"Savannah," Jennie said, in her squeaky voice, "aren't you supposed to be taking a class this break?"

Savannah rolled her eyes. "Just one. Just one more stupid class to finish my stupid degree –"

"A semester later than you were supposed to," Seth said, coming down the stairs. "Hey, Abs."

"Hey," she said. "Taking a break from the studying?"

"Just for food," he said. "Have to be on top of my game before Sadie gets here and tries to show me up with all that she thinks she knows."

Abby looked to Stu. "Sadie is... your cousin, right?"

"Yeah," he nodded. "Sadie and her brother, Jacob. They're both coming?," he asked his mother.

"Sure are," she smiled. "Jacob's almost done with college, just like you, Abby. And Sadie's in her first year of medical school. Studying sports medicine. And already interning with an NBA team as one of their athletic trainers and –"

"Yeah, because sweaty athletes are superior to dogs," Seth muttered.

"Probably pay better," Savannah pointed out.

"You'll love them both, Abby," Jess smiled.

"Dogs and NBA athletes?," Savannah asked.

"No, Sadie and Jacob," Stu said. "What about Kenji?"

"Cancelled at the last minute," Jess sighed.

"He's not going back to Japan for Christmas?," Sam asked.

"Nope," Jess sighed. "I'm telling you, that boy is NEVER going back to Okinawa. Matthew, Shoko, and Kimmie have to come all the way out here to see him. He hasn't been back once since he started college three years ago!"

"Who does he spend holidays with?," Seth asked, helping Sam to put the food on the table.

"Some friend from school," Jess answered. "A girl. And, no, they're not like that. I already asked. She's his roommate's girlfriend. Which sounds fishy to me, but whatever. What do I know, right?"

"You know how to cook the turkey until it's completely dry," Scott said.

"Scott! Stop eating! We've got to wait until the rest of the family is here, and –"

With that, the doorbell rang.

"I'll get it," Sean said, finally coming downstairs, a cell phone in his hand. "Hey, Abby. Congratulations."

"Thanks," she said to his back as he made his way to the door.

More shouts and squeals and general mayhem. Stuart looked over to Abby with a smile. "Big family. Kind of overwhelming, huh?"

But as she watched him, watching her... she thought it not even the slightest bit overwhelming at all. "Just perfect, Stu," she murmured, leaning in and kissing him before the next round of introductions began.

Stu

Dinner was... gross.

The meal itself was fantastic, and his extended family loved his bride-to-be. Abby had been chatting with Josh, Stu's uncle, about the student teaching she had ahead of her, and with Emily, Stu's aunt, about the wedding. As the conversations dimmed all around them, everyone could hear only Sadie and Seth, neither of whom would stop talking about medical issues, mainly trauma situations they'd seen on athletes and pets alike.

"Who knew," Scott said sarcastically, making a face of great surprise, after they'd all been sufficiently schooled in what rushing blood internally could do, "that hitting a dog with a car is the equivalent of kneeing some seven foot man in the crotch while you're going up for a rebound?"

"Well," Sadie said, "can't really knee a seven foot man in the crotch unless you're able to jump really high. Or, you know, you're really tall. Unfortunately, even at my height, most of those guys are crotch-level with my face. So, I guess I could head butt them in the junk and get the same kind of response."

"In the junk," Stu's dad, Nick, murmured. "Nice."

"We've raised up a real lady here, haven't we?," Josh laughed out loud, while Emily sighed.

Savannah grinned. "There's a really great joke about your face and some athlete's crotch just waiting to be said, Sadie, but I'm going to respect all the virginal ears at this table and not say it, even though –"

"Savannah," Sam shook his head at his sister.

"I was speaking clinically, Savannah," Sadie frowned. "And I can refrain from using the word 'junk' and use the more clinical words, like –"

"We get it, Sadie," Stu sighed. "We all get it."

"Well, anyway," she shrugged. "Those athletes are no different to me than those dogs are to Seth."

"All men are dogs," Scott affirmed. "Isn't that what you say in your book, Jennie? About how men only think about one thing? And the little women who marry them should be ready and willing to –"

She smiled demurely at him, even as she cut him off. "Did you read my book, Scott? I wrote it for sweet, young brides-to-be who are preparing themselves for godly marriages... not for jaded, hormone-driven pigs like yourself who no sane woman will ever marry."

Everyone at the table looked to her with varying degrees of shock. Even Sean couldn't hide his surprise that perfectly pleasant Jennie was... well, not perfectly pleasant.

"Well, golly, Jennie," Scott chortled out. "That's the most honest anyone here's been with me in a long time."

Jennie, just realizing what she'd said and what it could potentially do to her image, put her hand to her mouth and blushed very deeply. "Oh, y'all... I'm so sorry. I shouldn't have said that. Especially not during the season of Jesus's birth and all!"

"Technically," Stuart managed, "Jesus probably wasn't born on December 25th exactly, so…. you're good, I guess."

"You're awesome!," Scott laughed. "I like this new side of you, Jennie. A whole lot better than the way you're usually so –"

"Scott," Sam shook his head at his brother.

"Well, thank you, Scott," Jennie said. "I just…" She began to tear up. "Oh, I just think it's all the…" She looked to Sean.

And he smiled and gave her an understanding look. "I think it's all easily explained, Jen." He looked up at the rest of the family. "We wanted to surprise you all later, but now's as good a time as any. Jennie's a little more weepy than normal because… well, we're expecting."

A moment as the news descended on the crowd.

Then, Stu's mother burst into tears, and it seemed that everyone stood at once, trading hugs and congratulations all around. The louder it got, the closer Stu pulled Abby to his side, whispering in her ear, "First grandchild. Pretty thrilling, obviously."

"And how," Abby murmured, as Stu's mother practically danced around the table.

"We have to call everyone!," she shouted. "Jennie! We have to call all the family!"

Jennie nodded, beaming, as Sean went right back on his phone… with work. She only watched him leave the table as he kissed her forehead, then went right into calling up family members with his mother, dinner forgotten.

Stu ate while both sets of grandparents were called, while his mother's brother was called, while his dad's sister was called, and when his mother got on the phone with her good friend in Florida. Much squealing and crying commenced.

Abby looked at him with a smile. "Who is she talking to now?"

"Mrs. Hayes, probably," Stu sighed. "Her husband was our pastor for years. Up until I was a teenager. Then they moved out to Florida to another pastorate. But she and my mom." He held up his fingers and twisted them together. "Thick as gossipy, silly thieves."

Sam laughed at this.

"Oh, *no*, Chloe!," his mother cried out. "She can't be that *old*! Surely not! Well, my goodness. Eighteen, last week?" She covered up the phone with one hand and shouted over to Savannah, "Do you remember Faith Hayes?"

Savannah smiled slowly, coyly. "Oh. I remember. A few years ago, the lakehouse, me, Seth... Sam here, on leave. And Faith Hayes. I know Sam remembers." She looked over at him with a sly grin on her face.

Sam said nothing, staring down at his plate as he continued eating.

"Hey," Scott grinned, "sounds like there's a good story there."

"Oh, yeah," Savannah said. "But fairly chaste, given that we're talking about Sam, and given that Faith was probably only fifteen back then. But I remember a good deal of longing, lingering looks between the two of them, and if we'd been there more than a week, it would have –"

"Oh, that was a great week," their mother sighed again, having long since moved past her children's conversation. "Well, holy cow, Chloe, if Faith is that old, it'll be no time at all before you're calling me with news about a grandchild, too! And, hey, I can help get that process started with all the single sons I still have around here. Think Faith would be okay with me giving her number to Seth?"

Sam began choking on his turkey.

"Told you it was too dry," Scott observed, as Savannah whacked her brother on the back, smiling all the while.

"I'm too busy to date," Seth muttered.

"Guess that leaves Sam," Savannah said.

"Hey, I'm available, too, and I've seen pictures of that girl," Scott smiled, turning to face his mother. "Hey, Mom, tell her –"

And Sam reached across the table, grabbed his brother's shirt up in his hand, pulled him halfway across the table, and said, in a low, angry voice, "I will kill you with my bare hands if you touch Faith Hayes."

"Oh, and you could do it, too, couldn't you, big man?," Scott spat right back. "Which is something, I guess, since you can't be man enough to actually touch her yourself, right?"

"Fight, fight, fight!," Savannah began cheering.

"And," Stu whispered to Abby as mayhem broke out again, forcing his mother off the phone, as all the siblings began scuffling, Sadie began loudly proclaiming that she could do sutures on anyone who needed them afterwards, and Jennie began screeching about how the sweet baby Jesus was watching them all, "that concludes Christmas dinner at the Huntington household."

"I like it," Abby sighed, unable to hide her smile.

Abby

A spring wedding. Abby had said there wouldn't be time, that they needed to aim for a summer wedding, but Stu said three months was plenty of time to plan a wedding. His grandfather, who was ill but well enough to try to do the ceremony, told them he was all for a short engagement.

So, they made it happen.

On the Saturday before spring break, Abby found herself in the bridal room of the church Stu had grown up in, as her mother finished buttoning up the back of her dress for her, while Emily, Stu's aunt, went over the last minute checklist on her coordinator's clipboard, while Savannah fixed her lipstick (and kept pushing up her push up bra), while Rachel kept looking out in the hall for a glimpse of Seth in his tuxedo, and while Jennie sat in her maternity bridesmaid dress, fake-lamenting how *huge* she already was with those pesky twins in utero.

Yes. Twins.

"Jennie," Savannah said, still puckered up in front of the mirror, "leave it to you to do even pregnancy twice as well as everyone else."

"I'm not sure I'm doing it well," Jennie protested, dainty, sweet, and glowing in her gestation. Then smiling, "I'm just doubly blessed."

"Blessed," Rachel sighed. "Not as blessed as Abs, though. Did y'all see the gift Stu gave her after the rehearsal dinner last night?"

Rachel only knew half of the blessing. Abby had gone back to Stuart's apartment the night before, where most of her things had been moved from the dorm and were waiting to be unpacked. She'd had the urge to begin that process, fighting off the anticipation and the nerves that were already bombarding her now that the wedding was only twenty-four hours away. Stu had successfully navigated her away from the task, telling her that all she absolutely had to get done was to sit on the couch and unwrap the gift.

"Stu," she protested, "we weren't going to get each other gifts. It's a dumb tradition. We've already overspent on this wedding, and —"

"Your parents have overspent," he corrected. "We haven't spent a dime."

"You've spent more than a few dimes on the honeymoon," she chided.

"And worth every cent," he said, "as I can already feel the ocean breeze on my face and the sand between my toes." He grinned at her.

"Me, too," she sighed. Then, "I don't have a gift for you."

"I don't need anything," he said. "Nothing but you, sitting here, enjoying the gift that I got for you." And he got up from the couch, went into the bedroom, and came out a moment later with a beautifully wrapped package.

"You wrapped it and everything," she said.

"That I did," he said. "Used a whole roll of tape, too, so it might take you a while."

"Gift-wrapping will obviously fall under my list of responsibilities," she said, tugging at the bow, then at the paper, until she sat with a box in her hands.

Reaching over to break the tape at the sides, Stu lifted the lid and pushed aside the tissue paper, revealing a simple leather-bound Bible with a name embossed on the cover.

"Mrs. Abby Lynn Huntingon," she whispered, touching her new name and wiping away a tear.

"It gets better," he said, opening it up to the first few pages, showing her where their names were already recorded under "Marriages" with the next day's date written beside them.

"You have to marry me now," he shrugged. "It's clearly laid out for you in Scripture."

She laughed out loud at this, sighing and murmuring, "Come here," as she pulled him close and kissed him. "Stu, this is perfect."

"Yeah," he smiled. "Oh, and then there's this thing." He pulled a box from behind his back, opened it up, and laughed when she gasped at the diamond bracelet.

"The Bible would have been enough," she said.

"Scripture is sufficient," he nodded, putting the bracelet on her, closing the delicate clasp.

"And how," she said, "but wow, look at this."

"Conflict free diamonds, in case Jennie asks," he said. "Which she will, because all the other women will be looking to make sure I did right and bought you jewelry for the big day, and –"

"I don't care what all the other women are thinking," she said. "I don't care what anyone thinks. Ever. Just us."

"Just us," he smiled.

"Even still... I do like this bracelet," she grinned.

"Thought you might," he said, watching her quietly.

She took a deep breath. "Big day tomorrow, huh?"

"The biggest," he nodded. "It's going to be great. Every day, you know, from now on. Even when it doesn't seem great."

She smiled. "I can't imagine that every day won't seem great," she murmured, sliding closer to him. "I know what I'm getting into with you."

"Do you now?," he laughed, putting his arms around her.

"Yes," she said. "We're predictable. I'm going to teach, you're going to continue on schmoozing for money –"

"Unfortunately," he breathed.

"And," she said, hardly hearing him, "we're going to have a baby approximately five years from now, then another two years later."

"Then, no more," he said. "Six kids, two bathrooms, no good."

"Mmmhmm," she murmured. "Of course, before then, we'll have to find a place with two bathrooms."

"Yes," he said. "But that'll come. We'll leave it up to chance and fate to see how that works itself out, of course."

"Chance and fate," she said, kissing him. "Those would be excellent baby names."

He grinned. "Yeah." Then, more seriously, "I think whatever comes, whether we know it beforehand or God surprises us... we're going to be great, Abby. You and me, just like this."

"Just exactly like we are, right now," she agreed.

And he pulled her even closer and began to pray for the day ahead.

A day, she noted, that was beautiful and bright and full of hope. And she loved the way the bracelet he had put on her looked up against the dress her mother had now finished buttoning. Keeping the better gift to herself, she held up her wrist to the women gathered in the bridal room, anticipating their gasps of appreciation and blushing all the same as they rushed to her side for a better look.

"I wonder," Jennie mused, smiling at the bracelet without even asking about the origin of the diamonds, "why diamonds are always associated with love and marriage..."

"Maybe," Abby's mom mused, "because marriage is hard. That it takes years of irritation and grit and being hard pressed... to finally become something of value."

Everyone watched her with silent horror for a moment.

Abby sighed. It was the truth for her own parents, certainly. She remembered a happy home for the most part…. before her father's last pastorate. That little church, though, had changed them. Not just in ministry, which it forced them out of completely, but in their home, in their lives, in their hearts, and in the marriage that was made to hold it all together.

Abby didn't know how hard it had been. She had known how she herself had suffered through it at fourteen, but she couldn't have guessed what it had done to her parents. She knew, though, that they had gone through a lot and that her father wasn't who he had been. His hurts in ministry had changed him and transformed him, and they had affected her mother even more deeply. She was different now as well, aged, wounded…

… possibly stronger? Abby didn't know for sure, as she met her eyes, and her mother smiled.

"Marriage is hard," she said, "because life is hard. But you grow together, through conflict, through trouble, through trying times, together. And you come out stronger and better, and marriage? Is beautiful at the end, because you finally really know one another, and you've persevered, and you've changed… and you love one another, even still."

No one said anything for a moment… until Jennie burst into tears.

"Oh, *my!*," she yelled. "That is the sweetest thing I've ever heard! And so *true!* So very, very true, and I tell you it…"

Savannah rolled her eyes, even as Jennie continued blabbing on and on about the beauty of marriage, embracing Abby's mother as she did so, as Rachel herself wiped away a few tears, likely thinking of all the turmoil she'd gone through all these years, waiting for Seth to simply look her direction, loving him despite his cluelessness, even still –

"Don't listen," Savannah whispered in Abby's ear. "Because you and Stu? Won't have a day of trouble, girl. You already know just exactly what life with him will look like."

And Abby? Believed her entirely, even as she stood at the altar an hour later, hand in hand with Stuart, promising him forever, and facing a future that she could predict with certainty.

CHAPTER FOUR

Abby

Newlywed days turned into normal days, full of classes, work, and... life. Regular life.

There were harried, hurried days after the honeymoon, preparing for the end of her student teaching with the excitement of signing her first teaching contract. Then, there had been graduation and a summer position at their church, organizing and leading their children's summer programs. On top of it all was the thrill of coming home to him every night, learning how to be a wife, how to keep a home, how to keep a family, how to keep a happy husband.

And Stuart had work.

Exhausting, unfulfilling work.

Abby had known it before marriage, but she knew it more acutely after marriage when she was there to meet him at the door, to see the hollow look in his eyes and the strain of stress in his shoulders.

Distractions were good for Stu, after work like this. And Abby was good at distractions. She wondered sometimes if she could keep up the distractions until Stu retired from his hated job, his despised profession, the very career that sapped the life from him —

"Hey," he said, dejected, even as he came into the small apartment to find her waiting for him in the living room, where she quickly made her way to his side.

"Hey, Stu," she murmured, enthusiastically running one hand through his hair while looping her other arm around his neck, pressing against him, raising one thigh just so around his hip –

Abby was good at distractions.

"Well, welcome home to you, too," Stu managed a smile beneath her lips, his hands going straight to the bottom of her shirt, wandering their way up even as she pulled him closer. "Staying in tonight, are we?"

"Actually, no," she sighed, smiling at him. "We're going out."

"Then, that's a dirty move to pull, Abby," he groaned. "I'll go change clothes. Casual, right?"

"Yes," she said, following him into the second room of their two room apartment. It had seemed so much bigger back when she was dating Stu, but now that two people were living where only one should comfortably be able to live, she was surprised by how small it was.

No loss there, though, as this gave her an up close view of Stu stripping off the professional finery he wore every day.

"Where are we heading tonight?," he asked, tossing his jacket and tie to the bed.

"To Seth and Grant's place," she said. "Big announcement, they said."

Stu made a face at this.

"Yeah," Abby laughed. "The thought already crossed my mind, too. They're going to announce that they're marrying one another. Rachel will be crushed. But oddly reassured, as it'll explain why Seth has never given her a second glance."

"That's not it," Stu said, pulling off his shirt. "Seth likes women."

"Grant does, too," she murmured.

Stu raised his eyebrows at this. "Yeah, well, knowing the two of them, they've concocted some crazy scheme together that will get them in a load of trouble. I wouldn't be surprised if those idiots told us they'd found a treasure map and were setting off in search of lost gold."

"Big brother Stu, always looking out for Seth," she said.

"For him, for us... for those idiot politicians making it that much harder to get the money raised," he said. "Harder and harder every day to convince people to believe in ideology that I myself don't believe in, not when it's all pinned on men who are making the dumbest, biggest mistakes."

She swallowed at this, uncertain of what to say to make it better. "I'm sorry," she offered, walking up to him and pushing him back down onto the bed, crawling into his lap.

"I've got to get dressed, woman," he chided.

"No, you don't," she said, knowing this was a poor substitute for really hearing his heart, understanding what worried him, and meeting the need.

But she was afraid of what fixing the problem might do to the security of who they were, where they were, and where they were heading. So it was back to distractions.

"Abby," he murmured, lying back. "Treasure maps, pirate voyages, lost gold, yo ho, yo ho..."

"Grant and Seth can wait," she whispered. "All I want right now is you."

And Abby was certain that all that weighed on Stu could be forgotten, at least for now.

Stu

"This opportunity," Seth said enthusiastically as they all gathered around the table at his apartment an hour later, "is like a gold mine."

"Gold," Stu said, raising his eyebrows at Abby, who squeezed his thigh underneath the table.

Rachel continued pulling dishes out of the oven and off the stovetop, swishing around the kitchen pleasantly in a very short skirt while she glanced at Seth over her shoulder.

She hadn't changed in all the time Stu had known her.

"It's going to be great," she murmured. "And I think we're going to be really successful."

"Well," Abby said, "I think it's brilliant, Grant."

"Why, thank you, Abs," he grinned.

And it was brilliant. Grant and Rachel had pooled together the money left to them by their grandparents, along with money Seth had saved over the summers during college, and all three had plans to go into business together, opening the restaurant Grant had spent his life dreaming of owning.

They'd figured out a lot, but there were still holes in their plan.

"Now," Stu said, ever the concerned voice of reason, wanting to alert them to some of the most gaping holes, "when you say that things will be easier financially speaking when Seth is done with school, you mean... what exactly?"

"Seth will be paying the mortgage on the building at first," Grant said.

"With what?," Stu asked.

"With my practice," Seth grinned. "Remember old Dr. Jackson? The vet who always took care of our pets?"

"Yeah," Stu said, remembering the old man vaguely. He'd been old even when Stu was a teenager. "Did he finally offer you a job after all these years of volunteer work?"

"Better than that," Seth said, very nearly reading his brother's mind. "He's ancient. And he's well past needing to retire but has held on because he wants me to take over his client list. And he's selling me his clinic. Just told me yesterday. Just the kind of opportunity we've been praying for these past years, Stu. I won't go in as someone's assistant – I'll be doing all the major work from day one, all by myself."

Stu smiled to hear it. "Knew God would work something out. Congratulations, Seth."

"Well," Seth smiled, beaming in his brother's approval, "I'll still have to take out a loan for it all, but I'll be able to cover the payments for that and the mortgage for the restaurant. You know how much vets make? The good old doctor drives a Jaguar, Stu."

"You're going to be paying two mortgages," Stu said, considering something obvious that Seth, even in his veterinarian brilliance hadn't considered. "Where are you going to live? Once the lease is up here, since Grant's already said he's moving somewhere smaller to save on rent. Are you going to take out a third mortgage for yourself?"

Seth frowned at this. "Hadn't thought through that... I guess I could live at the restaurant. Maybe?"

Idiot.

"That'll all get worked out," Rachel smiled. Stu could just bet what Rachel's solution was. She'd moved out of her dorm after graduation and into a cute little house not far away, where she was paying her own mortgage comfortably. It would be no big deal at all for, you know, Seth to marry her, move in, and save himself the extra expense.

No big deal at all.

"Yeah," Grant nodded. "What's important now is making sure that we can turn a profit with the restaurant. Which is why we asked you two here. We need you to do a preliminary taste test for us."

Stu smiled over at Abby. "Dinner, cooked by someone else," she murmured, smiling back at him. "I'm all for that. Who did the cooking?"

"Grant," Rachel said. "All Grant. You remember how he cooks, Abs."

Stu watched as his wife took the plate Rachel offered her. "I might remember that. Though it's been a while."

"Not much kitchen space to cook in a dorm, you know," he said. "But there were a few meals back at my parents' house, remember?"

"Yeah," Abby sighed. "Your mother's immaculate kitchen. Didn't know you were the mastermind behind all of that food, though."

There was something in Grant's eyes as he looked over at her. But before Stu could wonder over it too long, Grant looked away from her and stood to bring a second plate over to the table. "Seth, you want in, too?"

"You bet," he said. "Haven't eaten all day."

"Poor baby," Rachel cooed. "Would've brought you something on my lunch break if I had known."

Stu opened his mouth to make a comment about this, but Grant cut him off with a lengthy explanation of the first dish, now in front of all three of them, as Rachel sat beside him and began taking notes.

Several courses and much conversation later, Grant grinned at them all as they concluded their suggestions, their praises, and their thoughts, all of which were positive.

"Well, we're not done," he said. "One more dessert to test out, if any of you have any room left."

Seth and Stu both groaned, already full, but Abby offered, "Always up for more dessert."

Rachel uncovered the dish, handed Grant a clean fork, and went right back to taking notes, even as Abby flushed at the sight of it.

Strawberry shortcake.

"Back in the kitchen, my mother's immaculate kitchen… yeah, I made it then, too," Grant offered, smiling at Abby.

Stu didn't know what to think as she blushed, and he didn't miss the wink Grant gave her as he poised the fork in her direction. "Tell me what you think, Abs," he said, even as she took the bite he offered, closed her eyes, and groaned appreciatively.

"Well?," Rachel asked, as Abby watched Grant for a moment. "How did it taste?"

"Familiar," Abby managed. "Strawberries. Like summer."

Seth made a face at this. "That doesn't make any sense. How can something taste like summer?"

Even as Abby blushed, Grant grinned wider. "Well, that was what I was going for, you know. Rachel, put it on the list."

And Abby wouldn't meet his eyes… but couldn't help but meet Stu's, even as he watched her with confusion and concern.

Abby

"So tell me about strawberries," he said later that night, just as she turned out the lights, just as he wrapped his arms around her in their bed.

"Strawberries?," she asked, yawning. "The dessert at Grant's place?"

"Yeah, that," he murmured, kissing the back of her neck.

"That's the second time I've had that dessert," she sighed. "He made it once when we were kids."

"When you were kids, huh?," Stu said, turning her around to face him. "Thought you didn't know Grant and Rachel until you were fourteen."

"Yes, well," she sighed, wrapping her arms around his neck, "fourteen is still a kid, you know?"

He smiled at this, leaning in to kiss her. "But didn't you date him when you –"

"Stu," she groaned. "Really?"

"Yeah, really," he nodded. "What was the big strawberry joke?"

"That's what we were eating the first time he kissed me, back in his mother's kitchen," she said. "There. Are you glad you know that now? Glad that you can picture it in your mind?"

"I'm not going to picture that in my mind," he murmured, leaning in to kiss her neck. "I have *way* better mental pictures of you to keep me occupied. Pictures that Grant wouldn't know anything about."

"I know," she sighed, smiling and relaxing.

"Even still, though," he said, stopping abruptly. "It was... a little inappropriate, huh?"

74

She blinked at him. "What was?"

"The way he fed you that dessert," he said. "With what it meant and all."

"I think you're overthinking it," she murmured against his lips. "I think Grant's just trying to do all that he can to make his dream a success. And kudos to him for having a dream, for enjoying what he does. It's a good and right thing, putting all of your energy and effort into something you're really passionate about. Yay for Grant," she concluded, pulling Stu closer and running her hands down his back, over his waist, down to his —

"Makes me wonder why I'm wasting my life in that stupid office," Stu said, completely unaffected by what she was doing.

"This again?," she asked. "Stu, honey, we've been over this again and again, and it —"

"It's just life," he said. "Just have to meet bills, save up, and live the... great American dream. I know."

Abby doubted that, though, as he placed a tender kiss to her lips and rolled over on his back, gathering her close enough to touch her but not enough to encourage anything else.

"I just wonder," he said, "what it would be like if I..."

"If you what, Stu?," she asked into the silence that followed.

And Stu had no answer for her that night.

Stu

In the morning, Stu had hope, for the first time in a long time.

He'd been thinking on it for a while. Ever since Abby's graduation, he'd been thinking about all that he missed before he'd taken the job that now made him miserable. He was a student, first and foremost, and he'd loved teaching. Before he'd left the university, he'd been told that doctoral work was a great option for him, with his speaking skills, his affinity for research, and his passion.

He found, though, that his passion had long since shifted from politics to... well, Christ. His greatest joy, apart from being with Abby, being married to her, revolved around the Bible study class he still taught at their church. He loved getting into the Scripture, explaining it, expositing it, and enabling others to live in its truth.

Given all of this, his thoughts drifted naturally to seminary. Very different from politics... but thrilling. So thrilling. Stu had spent part of the summer researching his options in this area and felt certain that the next step was seminary.

He approached the topic with Abby that next morning as they cleared away the breakfast dishes together, standing side by side at the sink, with him washing and her drying.

"I think I need to go back to school," he said, very simply. "I can't keep on with this job and... I need to go back to school."

"Doctoral work?," she asked, wrinkling her nose at him. "Stu, how's that going to put you in any different kind of position than where you already find yourself? It's not like these political action groups are looking for a PhD to suddenly move you beyond fundraising responsibilities or analyst jobs."

He didn't say anything for a moment, knowing what her reaction might potentially be. "Not doctoral work. I'm thinking about going to seminary."

And he saw it in her eyes. Fear, hurt, even betrayal.

Abby loved Christ. Abby loved the things of God. Abby loved Scripture.

But Abby didn't trust the church.

He knew pieces and snippets of her story, of her father's story. Abby
had told him long ago about the business meetings, the deacons who
tore him apart so as to keep the power in their small church, and the
depression that had settled onto her father like a heavy mantle after
months of anger, directed not towards those who had caused the
conflict but towards those in his home. He had seen the effect on her in
their own happy, healthy church, as she stayed away from anything
organizational in the church – meetings, committees, and the like –
even as she served with joy in the ministries of the church.

Stu could see what it had done to her. And he could see what it had
done to her father.

But apart from this one man, who had a painful ministry, Stu knew at
least a dozen others who were still serving, faithfully and with no
regrets.

Stu knew he would be the latter, not the former. Surely. If pastoral
ministry was even where he was going, because seminary could mean
teaching, administration, translation work…

But Abby's expression made it clear that there was only one natural
conclusion to seminary in her mind. It was all she knew, after all, as a
pastor's daughter.

"Seminary?," she managed, horror in her voice.

He sighed. "I knew you would react like this," he said.

"Well, yeah," she said, "since this is the first I've ever heard about any
calling to ministry." A pause. "Stu, are you feeling called to ministry?"

He ran his hands over his face. "I'm not sure. I feel like I'm called to do
something meaningful, and the older I get and the more I know Christ,

I'm entirely convinced that I need to move away from changing the world and focus on changing eternity."

"Maybe you can work with Sean," Abby offered. "I mean, he's got the social justice arm of his ministry, and you're clearly qualified to run that."

"I don't think," he said, glancing at her, "that my theology is nearly as... liberal, as my brother's. Not to say that he isn't Scripture-centered and all, but... I want to study. I want to study what God's Word says."

"So you can teach one day?," Abby asked, weakly.

And Stu could see it in her expression. That she knew full well that if Stu ever got into it, he'd likely end up in a pulpit. *That* was his gifting, communicating and speaking, and paired now with this great desire to be a theologian... well, it was a strong possibility. The thought of what this could do to their perfectly ordered future was clearly making Abby's stomach turn.

"I don't know," he said simply, trying to be reassuring. "But I know going to seminary is the next step." He swallowed. "I'll have to leave my job, take a night job, to do classes. It'll be a change, but... I think we can do it. I mean, if this is where God is leading us, we have to, right?"

And Abby simply nodded her head, turned away from him, and went right back to the dishes.

Abby

Ministry. It would look like this.

People everywhere, fake smiles galore, and never a moment's rest. People... smiling at you one minute, whispering that they loved you so much, plotting to destroy you the next minute, whispering in tight circles against you.

This was church ministry.

Abby swallowed at the scene before her.

The entire family had gathered at Sean's church that day to see the baby dedication service for the twins. The boys were three months old – just old enough to look around at the crowd gathered there for the big day, just little enough to keep from babbling through the entire sermon.

In other words, they were the perfect age. Which matched the perfect service Sean led. Which matched the perfect woman who stood at his side.

And the church people watched, with smiles and words of praise... but Abby could see beyond it, to the what ifs and maybes sinisterly lurking ever nearer and nearer to the optimistic Rev. and Mrs.

"How is she already so thin?," Savannah murmured to Sadie and Abby as they watched Jennie flit around the backyard cookout later, on the sprawling property that she and Sean had just, the spring before, built their dream home on. "Think she had a little nip and tuck done?"

"Probably doesn't have time to eat," Sadie responded. "She told me she's still nursing both of the boys, so she's burning twice the calories all the time without consuming the extra calories recommended for nursing just one. She knows the math, and she's using it to her advantage. Clearly."

"That," Abby said, sighing, "and she really doesn't have the time, like you said."

Savannah continued to watch Jennie, baffled. "How does she nurse both of them at the same time?"

Abby glanced over at her. "It's... possible. I guess. Right, Sadie?"

"Not that I know from experience," Sadie said, "but I did sit in on a lecture from La Leche, because that'll be super helpful in sports medicine and all, right? Anyway, they have this thing called the football hold." She demonstrated it on her own body. "She can put a boy in each hand, latch them on, and read a book, provided she can figure out how to turn the pages with her toes."

The very mental image this created left Abby thinking that she and Stu might never have children, honestly.

Savannah crinkled her nose at this. "Well, I guess that's efficient, one boy per boob, since she already has two of both—"

"What are you girls talking about?," Seth asked as he came up to stand with them, holding a plate full of food in his hands.

"Lactation," Sadie answered, her hands still mimicking that double football hold, just as Savannah answered with, "Jennie's ginormous, perfect boobs."

Seth nodded... then walked away.

"Dogs lactate, too, you know," Sadie called out after him. "And they're way more efficient than Jennie about it. I'm talking twelve puppies at once, some of them."

"Probably shouldn't have scandalized Seth like that," Abby said.

"Like he doesn't think about boobs already," Savannah scoffed. "He's a guy. And besides, he owes me after enduring life with five brothers and all the jokes I've heard over the years about their assorted body parts."

"I'm amazed by her," Abby continued.

"By Jennie?," Savannah asked. "How so?"

"Well, I'm amazed that she's handling all of this, all of these people, so well. And that she's able to get anything done at all. She told me that the twins aren't sleeping through the night and that she hasn't gotten any rest since they've been born, especially with Sean's work schedule.

Not that you can tell, with the way she has the house already decorated and spotless, all the time."

"And she's kept up all that she was doing with the churches before Nehemiah and Ezra came along, too." Savannah made a face. "Can you believe they picked those names?"

"I think," Stuart said, stepping up next to them, "that it's symbolic of what God's doing in their lives right now. Restoration, bringing people back to God, healing… the very things Sean has built his ministry on." He kissed Abby then looked over at his sister. "And you shouldn't be standing here being critical of them."

"I'm not critical," Savannah said, heatedly.

"She's actually been quite complimentary," Sadie said. "She said Jennie had perfect boobs."

Stu made a face at this.

"You haven't noticed?," Savannah asked.

"I haven't been looking," Stu frowned at her.

"Well," she said, dismissing him, "I'm just wondering why Jennie has to be so perfect all the time and – well, look at that. Just proving my point."

And Abby and Stu turned their attention to where Jennie was accepting Sean's rather passionate kiss with grace and flair, even pointing her little tiny foot up as she clung to him affectionately.

"She'll be pregnant again by Christmas," Savannah whispered. "Mark my words, Abby."

"Shh," Stu chided her, grinning, even as he pulled Abby close and Sean parted from his own wife, clearing his throat to speak to the crowd that had gathered there in the yard.

"Jen and I wanted to share some good news with you," Sean announced proudly, looking over to her.

"Geez, they're already pregnant again!," Savannah hissed at Abby.

"Our development team," Sean said, thankfully oblivious to his sister's rantings, "has been meeting and praying about what God would have next for Hope Church. And with the south and east campuses doing so well... well, we've been given a burden and what we feel is a green light from the Lord to begin plans for a north campus."

Murmurs of appreciation rippled through the crowds.

But Sean wasn't done.

"And I'm entirely convinced that the word I've received regarding the plant is that God already has a man to lead it."

Before Abby could wonder at the oddity of Sean relinquishing any control over a campus (he was killing himself running the two campuses of Hope Church himself, without any help), Sean looked their direction and smiled, actually choked up to say this.

"I want my brother, Stuart, to work alongside me."

Abby couldn't keep herself from glancing over at Stu, who kept a diplomatic smile on his face, even as his eyes communicated his own surprise to her.

Well. Wasn't this a nightmare.

Stu

He managed to get Sean alone thirty minutes later.

He'd always looked up to his oldest brother. Sean was in charge, focused, and a born leader. Personable, charismatic, and able to motivate people, he was a lot like Stuart himself was, with the added bonus of being completely unafraid to try anything, to go anywhere, and to be anyone. Jennie was cut from the exact same cloth, and the two of them together had always struck Stu as just what every ministry couple should be.

Maybe. Because it was entirely possible that not all ministries were the same and that different men were equipped differently so as to lead differently.

Not every place was Hope Church. And not every pastor was called to Hope Church.

And, on top of that, Stu reminded himself, not every man was called to be a pastor anyway.

"Hey, man," Sean said, "hope I didn't catch you by surprise with all that. But when God's doing something... you just go with it."

Stu took a deep breath at this. "Yeah, well... when God's doing something. But I'm not sure that this is what God's doing."

Sean looked over his head to wave goodbye to some church people. "Hey, come with me," he said, putting his arm around his brother's shoulders and leading him into the house. They tiptoed past the boys' rooms, which Jennie had decorated immaculately, of course. Stu smiled to see them, to catch a glimpse of his sleeping nephews tucked in, enjoying their naps.

Sean noted the look on his face as they finally got to his office. As he closed the door, he raised his eyebrows at Stu. "You and Abby thinking about starting your own family soon?"

"Uh, no... but thanks, Mom, for asking questions that are none of your business," Stu replied, smiling.

"Mom's been asking, huh?," Sean laughed. "She asked Jennie for five years, you know. And finally, BOOM! When God does what He's doing, He does it right, man. Two at once."

"You're very blessed," Stu nodded.

"Yeah, I still can't tell them apart. Nearly had a heart attack when Jen cut the hospital bracelets off of them. As long as she can tell who's who, I guess we're good," he said. Then, leaning forward, "About the church, Stu —"

"I don't know that this is where God is leading me," Stu began, in his best diplomatic voice. "Theologically speaking, we're worlds apart."

Sean considered this. "Both love Jesus, both believe the basics on most doctrine, both want to see lives changed —"

"Yeah, but there are some secondary issues that... I just don't know. We're working towards the same goals, of course, but I'm not sure we can work at them from the same place. You know?"

Sean waved his concerns away. "Different places. The north campus would be yours. I would only be executive pastor, not the preaching pastor or even the vision-caster for that campus."

Stu doubted very much that Sean would "only" be just an executive pastor. And even then, he was still the one leading the charge, pastoring the flock from afar, shaping the doctrine they taught and followed.

"Even still," Stu said, "I'm not all that certain that pastoral ministry is what I'm called to."

Sean sat back in his chair. "You are, brother. You totally are."

And Stu felt something at these words. An agreement in his spirit, at the words of his older, wiser brother, who was ahead of him on this road.

But still.

"I don't know," he sighed.

"Is it Abby?," Sean asked, playing with a paper clip on his desk. "Is she the one holding back on this?"

The simple answer was... maybe. Would Stu be able to embrace all that he thought he was being called to if Abby was on board? Would the call be a foregone conclusion if Abby had shown even a little enthusiasm about it? Would they be pursuing what was God's will for them if Abby had any interest in it?

Maybe.

"She's got some reservations," he said. "And for good reasons." He sighed. "As do I, of course. I don't know the first thing about being a pastor."

Sean watched him for a second. "You learn as you go. And Abby? Well..." He bit his lip for a moment. "Let me tell you something about Jennie. You know what first attracted me to her?"

Stu's mind drifted, very briefly, to the conversation between Sadie, Savannah, and Abby that he'd just barely caught and just what might have caught his brother's attention back when –

"Uh... well, she's very sweet," he said, ever the diplomat. "And beautiful. And she loves Jesus."

"And that's all great," Sean said, "but what I found most attractive about Jennie was how relentless she was. Knew it from the moment we met. I was interning at Grace, working my butt off for peanuts, and she walked in the front office, resume in hand, expecting that she'd get a job. A ministry job. Not even out of college yet and still completely assured that she'd walk out with the promise of a paycheck and better ministry experience than most people can ever get."

"And… she did," Stu smiled.

"Yeah," Sean laughed. "She did. Convinced them all that they needed her. And if she hadn't managed to do it that day, I know she'd have been back the next day, then the day after that, on and on until they hired her. I was sold, too. Knew before I knew anything about her that a woman like that, by my side? Would drive my ministry with all she had in her because it would be *our* ministry. She'd push me to be a better man, encourage me to always look for the next step up, and always be there, working just as hard."

"She does that," Stu nodded, appreciating anew this best part of Jennie, who made his brother look so good, so strong, and so capable, when half of the time, the credit he received was honestly hers.

"And I know," Sean sighed. "It's totally unromantic and all, but that? Was enough of a reason to pursue her at first. And then God took care of the rest." He paused for a moment, watching his brother. "I worry about how you'll do in ministry with Abby beside you."

Stu bristled at this slightly, at the implication that Abby was anything but just right for him. "Well, I won't do ministry without her."

"I'm not saying you should," Sean said. "I just… wonder, you know?"

And for the first time, Stu began to wonder, too. And he began, at least in part, to resent her just a little.

Abby

The crowds cleared out soon after. Stuart had spent the majority of that time accepting congratulations on a job he hadn't accepted, smiling and nodding graciously as he did so, reaching out to squeeze Abby's hand comfortingly from time to time as she walked alongside him.

"You guys heading home?," Scott asked, just as some of the last church people were making their way out to their cars.

"Not yet," Stu breathed. "I think we'll stay behind and help Sean and Jennie finish cleaning up."

Scott nodded, reaching out to hug Abby. "Give my best to EZ and Knee-high," he said. "I think they only spent ten minutes of their own party out here with the rest of us."

"She's got them sleep trained to nap during the hottest part of the day," Abby said, smiling up at her brother-in-law.

"Trained like dogs, huh?," Scott grinned. "There's something I never figured you could do with kids. Leave it to Jennie to do it, though."

And leave it to Jennie, Abby noted several minutes later as the two women were back in the house together, to have three month old twins contentedly having tummy time on the carpet together without a single fuss or noise.

"Sean and Stu should be done soon," Jennie said, smiling, as she sat next to Abby on the ground, reaching out and rubbing Ezra's fuzzy head as he continued chewing his fist and kicking his tiny feet. "Told Sean to clean up and clear everything out while there were still crowds here and he had more help, but he got caught up talking about the church."

Abby nodded at this, the millions of questions she wanted to ask about the church and this new turn with Stuart at the forefront of her mind.

Jennie seemed to sense it. "Stu seemed… surprised by Sean's offer."

Abby took a breath. "Well, we both were. Stu hasn't ever even… well, even expressed a desire to lead a church. Much less pastor one."

Jennie narrowed her eyes at this slightly. Then smiled away her confusion. "Well, it'll all get sorted out."

Abby was about to ask a question about this when Jennie reached out and touched her hand. "Abby, I just want you to know that you can call me… whenever, you know. Or just come by, anytime. I mean, I'm almost always here now with the twins, and just… anytime, okay?"

She wasn't sure if this offer was for Jennie's benefit or her own, if there was more that Jennie wasn't saying about either of them, but –

"All cleaned up, love," Sean said from the door where he and Stu were making their way back inside. He came to Jennie's side, reached out to kiss both boys on the heads, then lowered his lips to hers.

"Thanks," she murmured playfully. "Haven't gotten more than five minutes alone with you all day, Pastor."

"Sundays are awful," he acknowledged.

"And Mondays are worse," Stu said. "Abby and I better get going. I've got a full day of class, a full night of work –"

"And I've got both," she said. "Teaching and lesson planning."

"I've just got the boys," Jennie murmured.

And with that, Sean's phone rang.

"Sean, just let it go to voicemail," Jennie sighed.

"Can't," he said, turning the screen towards her so she could see who was calling. "More calls from the vision committee regarding that north campus. Gotta take it." He jumped up and waved to Stu and Abby, beginning his conversation even as he walked away.

Jennie's gaze followed him, and the disappointment in her eyes was almost physically felt, there in the room with them.

"Jennie," Stu said softly, "do you want us to hang around and help you get the boys ready for bed?"

"Oh, no," she said, quick to smile. "I'm good. I won't be able to walk you out now that Sean is occupied and someone has to watch the boys, but –"

"That's okay," Abby said, her throat suddenly tight as she remembered nights like this at her childhood home, where her father was always on call as a pastor. Always available to the very same people who had hurt them, always spending himself on people who didn't appreciate him.

"We'll go on then," Stu said. And they made their way out to their car silently and began the short drive home.

"Did you… tell Sean that you were hoping for a pastorate one day?," Abby asked after just a few miles, alarmed to hear the question herself.

"Well," Stu sighed, "we may have talked over what I saw coming next, after seminary, a time or two. Yes. You know what a big help he's been to me as I've been starting classes, figuring it all out."

He looked at her while she continued to stare straight ahead.

"Abby," he murmured.

"I'm just a little surprised," she said, tightly. "I mean, you've never even talked about it with me."

"Well, I didn't tell him I had any answers. That *we* had any answers. But I asked some questions, talked through some of my thoughts, just picked his brain. It would've been silly not to. I mean, I have a brother who's been very successful in ministry, who's walked this road of wondering about calling and all. Why wouldn't I talk to him about it all?"

"It just worries me," she said. "Worries me that we're heading towards…"

Towards just exactly what she feared the most. He'd started the classes, jumped into this world of ministry preparation… and he was happy. So blissfully happy. And Abby was scared witless about what it meant, about the direction it was taking them.

"We're not heading anywhere that we won't go together," Stu said, reaching out for her hand.

And the squeeze he gave was, for the first time, a smaller comfort than normal to Abby.

Stu

It was a rare night off for Stu, which meant that instead of concluding dinner and getting dressed for his entry-level job at the all-night shipping facility (where, ironically enough, he made more than he had as a political expert), he was able to go to bed and stay in bed with his wife for the entire night.

Unfortunately, this made little difference to Abby, who had endured a day of parent-teacher conference appointments and was completely exhausted. Not that Stu was trying to talk her into any kind of action, though. He was more intent on having what would likely be a difficult conversation with her before she could close her eyes.

"I had a church contact me," he said, thinking that the bluntest approach was the best.

"A church?," she asked, closing her eyes and curling into her pillow, even as Stu slipped his arms around her and kissed the back of her neck. "What for?"

"Word around seminary," he said softly. "Churches in the area looking for new pastors get connected to the preaching professors, resumes get handed around... you know."

"How do they even have your resume?," she asked. "And you only have one preaching class. You're a theology student."

"That's the thing," he said against her neck, smiling. "They've called me without a resume. And it was on the recommendation of that professor."

She let out a breath and turned to him. "Stu, you're scaring me."

"Scaring you?," he asked. "How?"

"When you said seminary, you didn't say anything definitive about church work. Or... pastoral work. I mean, you turned Sean down, right?"

"I did," he nodded. "But one no doesn't mean... no forever. And I didn't ever say that I wouldn't do pastoral work, Abby."

She glared at him. "Is that what they were calling for?"

"Well, yeah," he said. "They were looking for a pastor."

Abby sat straight up in bed. "And what did you tell them?"

"Well," he said, sitting up next to her, "after talking with them, I didn't get the sense that this was a place for us. They're very non-traditional, and you know me."

Conservative, traditional, reliable, maybe even too set in his ways. But this seemed to be a relief to Abby, as she laid back down and pulled him down with her.

"Good Stu," she sighed, relaxing into him, kissing his chest as she snuggled close to him.

"But you know," he said, snuggling into her, "it got me to thinking. Maybe, instead of this factory job, I could be doing a ministry job. You know, getting practical experience while I study, working more normal hours... you know?"

Her eyes popped open. "What are you saying?"

"I'm saying," he said, "that we should put my resume out there. In the school's resume service. And just see what happens. You know?"

Abby frowned. "I... I don't know, Stu."

She turned her back on him and didn't say another word.

Abby

He was standing in the front of the church, leading a business meeting.

He was well versed on how to do this. He had done it countless times before in his first pastorate, then a handful of times at this one. But as he stood there on that evening, her father discovered something – not all churches are the same.

This issue was a minor one. Something so insignificant and inconsequential that it shouldn't have garnered any discussion. But tensions were high, emotions were everywhere, and people? People were fallen. Even good church people.

Especially good church people.

Abby hadn't wanted to stay in the service once the yelling began. And if her mother had been thinking clearly, she would have sent all three of her children out. But as it was, none of them were thinking clearly, given the direction the conversation was heading in the county seat church.

"I think," one of the angrier deacons had begun yelling, "that we call a vote to see if there's any trust left in Brother Mike!" He glared at her father.

Another voice rose from farther back in the pews, calling for reason and asking that they all stop and pray it out, only to be drowned out by a woman from the opposite side of the room, who stood and screeched at him.

"We're done praying!," she said. "I've gone to this church my entire life! My parents went here. My grandparents went here. And, Pastor, I was here when you got here, and I will be here when you leave."

A chilling prospect actually, more so for the church than the pastoral family, but Abby hadn't known it then. What would they do if he lost his job? Where could they go in town without people talking about them? What about her school, her friends?

What about her dad, who looked almost sick as he steered the meeting back on course for that night, knowing surely that this wouldn't be the end, and...

Abby's throat clenched to see that it wasn't her father who stood before the church now. It was Stu. And as he called for reason, in his calm, thoughtful way, she saw the light leave his eyes, his passion for Christ dwindle, and his hope extinguish.

Just like it had with her father.

This wasn't the future she had wanted. For him. For their marriage. For herself.

"Abby, Abby, hey..."

His voice called her out of the nightmare, and before she could open her eyes, she realized she was sobbing. Stu gathered her closer than he had already been holding her, and she wound her arms around him, unable to stop crying.

"Abby, what's wrong?," he whispered.

"Stu," she sobbed. "Bad dreams. So, so bad..."

"Hey," he soothed, holding her with one arm, putting his free hand to her face, "just dreams. This is real. You and me, okay here, happy here, right? What can I do to make it better?"

Forget this crazy idea. Just be okay with life like it was. Abandon this pipe dream of changing eternity –

"Stu," she pleaded, "I just need you. I need you."

He was all she needed. Him, far from a pulpit, far from angry business meetings, far from ministry.

He misunderstood her meaning and took her mouth with his. And the more his hands swept over her and he drew her closer, the more she was convinced that he hadn't misunderstood her. She needed him, like this. More of him. Him completely.

"Stu," she managed, breathing him in and dispelling what was left of the lingering nightmare.

She woke up the next morning, and the first coherent thought she had was that Stu had magic hands. Wonderfully soothing and calming, as he continued to trail his fingers from her hip to her knee, then back again, slowly and teasingly, again and again... while he sat up in bed, glasses on, reading a systematic theology textbook, she noted, when she opened her eyes to him.

"Hi," she breathed out, only slightly annoyed to see his attention split... but mostly just pleased to see his intent, studying face. This was the same Stu she'd fallen for, back in that Poli Sci section.

"Hey," he breathed, putting his book back on the bedside table, gathering her close. "You doing better this morning?"

"Yeah," she said. "I'm just... apprehensive."

He nodded, acting as though he knew when clearly he couldn't. He hadn't lived through it like she had.

"About... church? A job in a church?," he asked.

"No, Stu," she sighed, just a little exasperated. "About the disappearing rainforests. Yes! The church thing!"

He grinned. "Just wanted to make sure we're on the same page," he murmured.

"Sweetheart, I don't think we *are* on the same page with this," she whispered.

"I'm not jumping into something tomorrow," he said. "We would be wise about it, Abby."

"I know," she sighed. "I know. But, Stu," she moaned, even as she stroked his face, "pastoral ministry? This is actually crazier than joining the circus."

He laughed. "How? How is this crazier?"

"You don't know pastoral ministry. Wild animals and carnies have nothing on deacons and little old church widows."

"Abby Lynn Huntington," he scolded, giving her a face of mock shock.

"Uggggggghhhh," she sighed, putting her hands to her face, even as he moved over her, still grinning. She couldn't think when he looked at her like that, with his calm, reassuring smile. Church ministry. Ugh. Church ministry.

But Stuart, smiling at her, looking hopeful for the first time in a long time...

"Okay, Stu," she said, finally resigned to this, praying that God wouldn't work it out. Praying that God would smash Stu's dreams to pieces. "We'll do what you think is right." She frowned at him, lacing her arms around his neck. "Now, properly wake me up… Pastor. Ugh."

And before she could quell the anxiety even the joke of a name brought up in her, Stu laughed out loud, lowered himself to her and whispered, "Yes, ma'am."

CHAPTER FIVE

Stu

He sent out 79 resumes to area churches that fall and heard back from three.

And those three simply wrote to tell him that he was out of the running.

Stu was beginning to think there was something deficient in what he had been doing in just waiting and seeing what would happen. He was young, which most congregations seemed to like, but he was inexperienced, which most congregations didn't seem to like. He had a graduate degree already, which most congregations seemed to like, but he was just barely into his seminary studies, which most congregations didn't seem to like. About all that these diverse churches seemed to agree on was that he couldn't expect to be paid much at all.

He had expected as much.

And Abby? Seemed content that nothing was working out.

Until the day they got the call from the small church just an hour's drive away.

"Hello?" Stu answered the phone that morning before Abby left for work. "This is he." She turned to look at him and saw his eyes grow wide. "Oh, good morning!" He stood up and began wildly gesturing to her, while mouthing, "CHURCH! CHURCH!" She put her purse down and walked to his side, putting her ear next to the backside of his phone, straining to hear what was being said.

"Well, we've got your resume here and just wanted to make sure you haven't taken a position with another church."

She saw the unwritten statement in Stuart's eyes in her peripheral vision. *As a matter of fact, I haven't because YOU, dear sir, are the first to call me back.* "No, sir," Stu said clearly, "I'm still looking."

The gentleman cleared his throat. "Good, good. I don't suppose you'd be available to drive down next weekend and preach on Sunday morning?"

It didn't really matter what was on their schedule for that weekend. He would clear it, drive the distance, and be just thrilled to do so.

"Yes, sir, I'm sure I could make that happen."

"Great. You'll need our address. Got a pencil handy?"

Stu turned so quickly that he knocked Abby in the head with the broad side of the phone. "Ouch," she mouthed at him, irritably, as he grimaced on her behalf, reached out to kiss her head, and began looking around the kitchen for a pen. She pulled one out of her purse, and he held out his free hand to write on, winking at her as he did so.

"Yes, sir. I sure do."

Stu chatted with the gentleman a few more moments, wrote down the address, and thanked him, saying that they would be there in a few days. He hung up the phone, turned to her, and said, grinning from ear to ear, "Well, there you go."

"Stu," she sighed as she watched him warily. "A church. Full-time?"

"Yes!"

"Do we know anything about the church?"

"No."

"Do we know anything about the town?"

"No."

Even so, he was thrilled. He could only manage to sleep for a few hours after she left for work, so excited and eager to find out all that he could about this potential new church. So, he researched most of the afternoon, had it all organized, and was ready to share it all with Abby just as soon as she came back home.

Surprisingly, there wasn't much to share.

"Wow... this is it?" She looked over the information he'd compiled, a frown on her face.

"Yeah," he said. "It looks like there are only 800 people in the town."

She nodded. "Just one church then?"

"No, actually. Three churches. And, surprisingly enough, all of them are the same denomination."

"That seems kind of strange and... terrifying," she said, her expression attempting to communicate several things.

None of which he got.

"I think," he told her, still grinning, even as he pushed aside his computer and the very little information it had given them, "that things are going to work out just fine." He pulled her into his arms enthusiastically and gave her a kiss that she could feel from the top of her head to the tips of her toes. "Isn't this exciting?"

"Maybe," she said, keeping her thoughts to herself even as she let him pull her closer.

Abby

They drove in an hour early on Sunday morning so that they could drive around town and "take it all in," as Stu had suggested.

Abby had reluctantly and stoically agreed, as she had to every suggestion he had in this terrifying new venture. Even as she sat in the passenger seat, her hands clutched together tightly, she watched, horrified, as the interstate gave way to a two lane road, then to a simple blacktop road, and as all signs of civilization fell away around them.

Great place, Stu.

Still, she reminded herself to bite her tongue as they approached the town. They passed the city limits sign... then, nothing.

Three miles later, she turned around and looked out the back window of the car. "Was that it?"

Stu shook his head. "Surely not... there wasn't anything there!"

On they drove, until they saw the city limits sign for a *different* town. Abby suppressed a sigh of defeat.

"Well, I'll be," Stu said, in an exaggerated drawl, befitting where they now found themselves, "that *was* the town!" He turned the car back around, and they headed back the way they had come, slowing down to a crawl as they entered the city limits for a second time. Sure enough, a tiny little sign on the main road indicated a secondary road passing through town. They turned onto it and immediately saw a beautiful little church, a small convenience store, and a lone fire engine.

"Is that... it?" Stu looked over at her, still clearly puzzled.

"I have no idea." She checked the address, concerned, and looked back at the church, confirming that they were indeed in the right spot.

"What about the other churches? What about the school?," Stu asked, very nearly pleading with her to tell him that this wasn't all there was to their probable future home.

Abby wasn't going to live here. No way.

But she kept her thoughts to herself, wanting so desperately to be the supportive, encouraging wife Jennie's book challenged her to be (yes, she had resorted to reading the book), the supportive, encouraging wife that Jennie would be if Sean drove her out to the middle of nowhere and expected her to make ministry magic.

As if.

"Maybe you should try a different road, Stu," she said, reaching over to rub his knee. There. Encouragement.

It seemed to work. "Okay, let's try this one." He maneuvered the car onto a graveled path, which appeared to be tapering off into a dirt road but then mysteriously became another paved road on which sat a fairly large school building.

"Grades K-12," she read out loud off the sign. "All in one building. Have you ever seen something like that?"

He shook his head, then his expression softened. "Hey, look at that!" She followed his gaze to a sub-division of slightly newer homes, nestled up next to an older neighborhood full of homes with sprawling porches. Nearby was another church, smaller than the one they had just seen.

"Well, this seems... nice," she lied.

"It does, doesn't it?," he asked before turning the car back around and heading towards the first church they had seen, the church where he would be preaching.

Sure enough, as soon as they pulled into the parking lot, an older gentleman came out from the church and walked over to their car to meet them. Stuart stepped out first, held out his hand, and gave a winning smile. A fundraiser's smile, Abby noted. Ever the politician, even for Jesus.

"You Stuart?," the gentleman asked.

"Yes, sir," Stu answered. "Though you should feel free to call me Stu."

"Brother Stu," the stranger nodded.

Oh, good grief. It was that kind of church. Abby mentally fought against the remembrance of all those people yelling for "Brother Mike" to step down, and –

"Hmm." The gentleman's lips tightened. "You're younger than I expected."

Abby stood there silently as he scrutinized "Brother Stu" without even noticing her. The awkward moment was at least partially broken as Stu put his arm around her and said, "And this is my wife, Abby."

The gentleman looked him over again. "You're old enough to be married?"

Didn't Stuart put his birthdate on his resume? Abby was certain that he had, but perhaps the math was too complicated for their impolite friend, who even now watched them warily as if they were two teenagers fresh out of high school.

"Yes, sir," Stuart said with a laugh. "And your name is...?"

The gentleman sighed. "Horace." A moment passed. "Well, no need in us standing out here in the cold. You two come on in and see the church." Stuart squeezed Abby's hand in his as he led her across the parking lot, his attempts at small talk all but lost on their most unwilling host.

After a quick and silent trip around the small church, Horace left Stu to prepare. Before he exited the building, he turned around and looked at her. "Abby, was it?" He regarded her with curiosity.

She managed to answer with a polite, "Yes, sir?"

"Do you play the piano?"

She nodded. You didn't grow up as a PK without picking up a few skills. "Yeah, a little."

He nodded to himself, muttering, "Well, that's something, at least." And then, he was gone.

Abby turned on her heel, gave Stu a look, and opened her mouth to say many impolite things –

But he stopped her with a smile and an insistent, "Stay open-minded, Abby. Just one person."

Just one person in one tiny town and… she nodded, biting back all that she would have liked to say. With a pat to his shoulder (ever the encourager, thus saith Jennie), she left Stu alone to review his notes, choosing to walk the building and pray, willing herself to calm down with every footfall.

This church didn't look much like the church her father had left nearly a decade ago… but she could still feel the panic rising up in her heart. Something about a church, any church, did this to her.

She fought against the urge to run away screaming.

The urge only increased when the crowds came. It looked as though the whole town had come out to see the new guy, to give their thoughts and opinions, to watch Abby and Stu both as they shook hands and fielded names and smiled politely. Then, Stu stood to preach...

... and Abby lost just about every ounce of hope she'd had.

He was doing what he was made to do. He was where he was created to be. He was going to pastor a church, probably like this one, probably just exactly like this one.

She couldn't keep her eyes from good old Horace, who sat on the front pew with his arms crossed during the entirety of the service, and his posture brought to memory the angry business meetings of years ago. The yelling, the crying, the shame of it all – so overwhelming, so terrifying, and so completely *not* what she would *ever* tolerate ever again –

She felt the pressure of Stu sitting down next to her, draping his arm over her shoulder, wordlessly seeking affirmation for what he had just done, for what he was about to do to them.

And Abby could only manage a tiny squeeze to his knee as she wiped away a tear.

Stu

After the service, Horace approached Stuart with the first smile they had seen him give. A tentative, slight smile, but a smile nonetheless. "Good job," he told him, even as a young woman elbowed her way into the conversation, reaching out for Abby.

"Hi!," she trilled enthusiastically. "My name is Shannon! You must be Abby!"

"Yeah," Abby answered, smiling just slightly, the tension in her face obvious to Stu, if to no one else.

"Geez, Horace," Shannon continued on. "Did you see the crowd today? It's like the old days, y'all. I think everyone was just really touched and inspired by your sermon, Stu."

Before he could respond, Horace cleared his throat. "We've got lunch for you two with the search committee, if you're up for it."

And Stu squeezed Abby's hand even as he spoke for them both without asking her. "Of course."

There were introductions, quickly made, all around. There was Merle, a senior adult who had to be in his eighties. He was a retired Marine and informed Stuart, while introducing himself, that he had insisted that the church find a seminary-educated man. As soon as this was out of his mouth, he went on to ask Stu what he thought about the importance of a seminary education. Before Stu could navigate this minefield discussion (as there was the issue of Stu just barely into the waters of seminary himself), a woman their mothers' age interrupted him, giving Stu a warm hug, introducing herself as Helen, and telling him how she so hoped having him as her pastor would bring more "young people like you" into the church. She pulled her husband, Tom, into the conversation, insisting that they had *many* ideas on what might work in bringing in more visitors. Shannon re-introduced herself to Stu and Abby again, telling them (again) that the sermon was far more interesting than any sermon the last pastor had ever preached. At this, Helen slightly averted her eyes and Merle's face furrowed even more deeply. Tom took Stu's hand next, breaking the moment by telling the newcomers about how long they had been looking for their new pastor.

A full year.

"Yeah, a whole year we've been meeting together, trying to find the right man," Horace said, with a sigh. "I hope we'll all go to bed tonight knowing that the job is done."

Stu and Abby exchanged a quick glance again, wondering at how fast this was moving. "Well," Stuart offered diplomatically, "I can agree to finding resolution for your church. But are you planning on taking a vote tonight?"

"Why wait, if it's just that clear what God is doing?," Merle offered.

Why indeed, Stu thought, as he saw the terror multiply exponentially in his wife's eyes.

And so the meal, complete with many things left unsaid, began, and with it, everyone began sharing their life stories. Merle was active in the local seniors' group, and when he wasn't spending his time sorting all that out, he could be found at the drug store, drinking coffee with all the other senior adult men in town. Helen was a nurse at the hospital two towns over. "A labor and delivery nurse!," she clarified in Abby's direction. "I work with the best OB in the area, honey. I'll be sure and get you his office number. You know, for when you and Stu need it."

Abby very nearly choked on her assortment of casserole dishes at this, but Stu smiled broadly and thanked her in advance.

Helen's husband, Tom, owned the town's only construction business and would have to leave in another hour to get to a project the next town over. Shannon owned the town's beauty shop, a "cute little house" Helen informed them, right next to the school.

"I was there this morning," Shannon said, "checking on a leak in the roof. Older houses require so much maintenance! Tom, I might need to have some of your guys out there to give me an estimate on fixing up some problems."

Tom nodded, as Shannon continued. "And I saw a little red car that I didn't recognize drive by while I was there... was that y'all?"

Stuart smiled a bit awkwardly. "Yes, that was us." A pause. "What do you mean, a car you didn't recognize?"

The whole table exchanged smiles, and Shannon patted his hand, "Oh, we know *everyone* here in town. You can't drive through Main Street without it being front page news the next day. That's just part of living in a small town."

This earned Stu another tight smile from Abby.

"So, Stu," Shannon began, "tell us about the two of you. How did you get into ministry?"

Before Abby could tell them that, actually, they weren't into anything, Stuart interrupted her. "Well, we both come from ministry families. My grandfather was a pastor, my brother's a pastor, and Abby's dad was a pastor as well."

She shot him a look that no one else seemed to notice.

Helen clasped her hands together. "Oh, Abby! A PK! How wonderful! Where does your father pastor now?"

Abby tore her eyes from Stu, then cleared her throat delicately, "He doesn't pastor anywhere, actually."

"In between pastorates?," Shannon asked, cutting up her food.

"No," Abby said simply. "Run out of his last pastorate. Quite maliciously, in fact. And he hasn't even become a member of a church anywhere since. I think the last time he was in church was... well, the day I married Stu."

All eyes of the committee members were on her now. No one said anything for a moment... until Stu spoke up.

"Well, all of Abby's extended family is in ministry. She has an aunt and uncle who are missionaries in Costa Rica with the denomination's board."

"Oh, I should write this down," Helen said, excited. "We have a prayer night at the church and are always looking for missionary names. You know, so we can pray for them better." She pulled a pen and an old receipt out of her purse. "What are their names, Abby?"

"Bryan and Christy Murphy," she said. "They've been in Costa Rica for... well, forever, actually. Though there was a three year appointment they did in Africa alongside friends of theirs." She smiled begrudgingly over at Stu, thinking about this branch of her family, still in ministry and still very much in love with Christ. Maybe all ministry wasn't bad, if her overseas family was an accurate representation. "One of my cousins was actually born there in Namibia. They call him their little African-American."

Blank stares all around.

"Which is funny, you know," she said, "since he's as white as me." More blank stares. "Actually, more white because he has no rhythm."

Stu laughed at this, but everyone else just exchanged troubled looks.

"Well, that's a horrible thing for any parent to say about their child," Merle managed, frowning.

"Oh, Abby's the one saying he has no rhythm," Stu joked, trying to deflect the tension that had crept into the room. "Not his parents."

"I'm talking about the African American part!"

Shannon rolled her eyes, "Oh, Merle," she began, somewhat exasperated. "African American people are just wonderful. " She nodded to Abby. "I've met a few in my time, you know. And they have such a nice church on the other side of town."

Helen nodded her head and patted Abby's hand maternally. "Yes, but dear, you don't need to go over there. " Then, she practically whispered, "Dangerous, you know. They're just not like us."

Before Abby could hear any more that might potentially set her off on these people, Stu put a hand to her knee, and she responded by turning the conversation back to him. "Well, enough about me," she said. "Stu, you should tell them about where you're from."

Stu nodded, "Fort Worth. Just down the road a little ways."

Merle nodded approvingly, Helen smiled, and Tom said, "I've been there before. Dallas, too."

"Oh," Shannon said. "I love the shopping there!"

"It is nice," Abby affirmed, and Stu almost applauded her effort to finally be positive.

"It really is! Of course, it's not like here. The city, the smog, and... well, you know." She lowered her voice a bit. "All of those people."

"Yeah," Stu said, "it does get a bit crowded."

"I'm telling you, one time when I was there I saw the *craziest* thing!," Shannon continued. "This woman was there, totally and completely covered up in this black robe thing. Oh, Helen, what do they call those things?"

Helen, obviously considered a woman of the world since she worked in the big city two towns over, stated it with exaggerated importance. "A burr-kuh, dear."

"Yes!," Shannon looked at Abby, practically slamming her hand on the table. "A big black burr-kuh! Just her eyes showing! In July! In Texas! I tell you, it was the weirdest thing ever. And then her husband," her contempt became even more evident at this point, "he was just wearing short sleeves and jeans, and I wanted to tell him, 'Do you have any idea how *hot* your wife is dressed like that?! Why do you force her to do that?!' Crazy, I tell you. And then I spent the rest of the trip worrying that they were *terrorists*, and I just couldn't even relax. Had to cut my trip to the mall short that day." She sighed and was joined by a few others at the table, who seemed to understand and empathize with her frustration at an increasingly complicated world outside the city limits.

Stu saw Abby take in a deep breath, likely to begin a discussion about the beliefs of Islam and how when it came to modesty and Biblical headship in the family, they probably had it more right than mainstream evangelical Christian culture (gasp!), but he saved her from stringing up her own noose (and his as well) by asking, "What can you tell us about the church?"

Horace, who had been silent throughout the whole meal, spoke up. "We're just a simple, small town church. The people here are really good people, hard working people, kind people."

Helen nodded affirmingly, patting Abby's hand again, smiling at Horace. "They are. You'll love the town. The church is actually the oldest building in the community, believe it or not. Over one hundred years old and the very social center of town. Practically everyone goes here!"

"Well, that's not entirely true, Helen," Horace interjected. "They either go here, or to the—" he paused to censor himself "— the African American church." The other members smiled at this, as if to say, *Of course!* "Or they go to Freedom Church."

Everyone seemed to freeze mid-bite. "Freedom Church?," Stu asked. "Is that the church by the school?"

Tom nodded. "Yeah… it was started about five years ago. Kind of like a… well, a mission church of ours."

The others quickly nodded. Stu grinned. "Wow! A mission church! I've never heard of a church this size establishing a mission church. Very impressive."

Helen smiled, very eager to impress them. "Oh, it is! Half our congregation left with the pastor five years ago and started that church over there. It's still growing!"

Though he had never known anything like it himself in all of his years in church, Stu could read between the lines. He heard what hadn't been said. It was a church split. He glanced over at Abby, saw that she heard the unspoken words, too, and saw the horror on her face. Even still, though, he smiled past his misgivings and began asking more about the community, about the needs, about what God was doing in this small place.

He wasn't ready to give up on these people. Maybe, just maybe, they would come back here and make this a forever kind of deal.

Abby

They were *not* coming back here. Ever.

If the comments indicating the small-mindedness of the people weren't enough to scare Stu off, then surely the indication of a church split would be.

Abby could visualize the business meetings that had probably taken place. She could picture them in her mind, could imagine what had driven the process forward. Yelling, fighting, gossip, and slander, likely directed at the pastor. This pastor had gone on to thrive since then, in a new place and ministry... but what had happened to the men who had come after him to *this* church?

Abby knew without seeing their faces herself. They'd been eaten alive by a hurt church, a fighting church, a church still dealing with the wounds of conflict.

Stu would *not* be eaten alive by them as well. And neither would she.

As the meal concluded and Abby tried to figure out a way to get Stu alone to talk over these things, wordlessly communicating the great need to him by squeezing his thigh so tightly that she was certain he would be bruised in the morning, Shannon clasped her hand enthusiastically.

"Have y'all got a few minutes to come with us?"

Before Abby could answer, Stu smiled and answered for them both (again) without asking her (again). "Sure. Where to?"

Tom held up a set of keys and grinned back at him. "The parsonage."

Of course. This was a parsonage church. Because what would be better for Brother Stu and Sister Abby than living in a house literally footsteps away from the church, where Stu would be on call all day and all night for all kinds of crazy insanity and –

"You know," Helen said, "just to help you feel more at ease about making a decision, getting to see where you'll live."

Though Abby was certain that nothing would make her feel any ease at all about any of this... well, Helen was right. As soon as they walked across the street and Tom unlocked the door to the nice brick home, Abby began to feel... well, just slightly more at ease about everything.

Slightly.

She chided herself for being so fickle. Up and down in her emotions in all of this, fighting mad one moment, emotional the next –

Stu stepped in behind her, still holding her hand, as she took a deep breath.

A home. A real home. The house wasn't huge by any means, but she felt like breaking into song about how they were "movin' on up" as soon as she sauntered into the spacious front hall. After years of dorm living and months now in an apartment much too small for two people, this felt like enough. A real home.

Two bathrooms. Just like they'd said they'd have one day.

They toured each room, looked over the backyard, and saw the garage. Tom and Helen took Stuart aside to talk with him about the yard maintenance the church had been hiring out in the interim, leaving Abby alone with Shannon.

Shannon waited for a long moment before speaking, her eyes roaming the living room. "We painted this place after the last pastor moved on." She bit her lip and seemed to consider her words. "He wasn't… a good fit for the church. It was good that he moved on."

Abby said nothing at this confirmation. Even still, there were a lot of unknowns about the whys behind it. Had it been the church, had it been the pastor, had it just been a bad fit, or had it been something worse? So many questions, not many answers, and Abby really needed to talk with Stu –

"Anyway," Shannon said, oblivious to all that Abby was thinking, "the ladies and I thought the inside needed a little maintenance. Half of the church wanted to wait until we got a pastor so that he and his wife could have some input on the color and all, but I just couldn't bear the thought of keeping *gray* walls a minute longer."

Abby looked around at the creamy beige earth tone Shannon had picked and had to agree that it was a vast improvement over gray.

"The house is wonderful," Abby told her, meaning it, meaning this much at least.

Shannon feigned breathing a sigh of relief, and Abby smiled, liking this woman in spite of all of her suspicions and fears. "I'm so glad to hear you say that." A pause, then, "We *really* enjoyed having y'all here today. I think Stuart would be a wonderful fit for our church."

Abby nodded, not sure what to say, clearly feeling conflicted. In the extended silence, Shannon seemed to be wrestling with whether or not to say anything else, but after a moment, she finally spoke. "It was a church split, you know," she said, clearly thinking that Abby didn't know or hadn't already deduced this from what little they had been told over lunch.

"Oh?," Abby managed.

She came closer, speaking in a lower voice, as if she were afraid someone might hear. "Half the church left to go to Freedom Church. It all but destroyed what we had going when the pastor left, and we've had a revolving door of interims in and out ever since. And we've tried. We've tried to make it work out with other pastors, but the church is hurt, we're all hurt, and… it's just been really hard."

She didn't let Abby in on any other details, leaving her to simply wonder about the tumultuous times they had been through.

"It's been really lonely for people our age," she indicated Abby as part of the group, then balked at that. "Well, listen to me saying that, and you're probably a good ten years younger than me!" Likely fifteen. But Abby wasn't going to press the point. "But even with that difference, having you and Stuart here is just a breath of fresh air. I felt today in church, for the first time in a long time, that things might start looking up again for us."

She hesitated for a moment, only a moment, before blurting out, "My husband doesn't go to church, you know."

Abby didn't know what to say to this, at this woman's inclination to share so much of her heart so soon. "He doesn't?"

She shook her head. "He did, you know. Back before the split. But he doesn't anymore. Which is okay because I make do." She looked at Abby with hopeful eyes. "But I really think, with a new young couple like y'all here, he might be encouraged to start coming, after all of these years. Then, I think my kids might get more serious about it. They were telling me after church today how much they liked the stories Stuart told, and I just… "

She faltered off for a moment, seeming to search for the right thing to say. "When you said what you said about your dad... I can relate, you know? Jeff, that's my husband, was hurt, just like that. And he's left the church, but I think, if the right people were here, that..."

She wiped away a few tears, as Abby's heart clenched. "I just think y'all should come here," she said softly.

Before Abby could think of an appropriate response, the front door opened, and they could hear Helen, Tom, and Stuart making their way back in the door. Shannon smiled a secretive smile at Abby and squeezed her hand as though they were lifelong friends.

"What are you gals gabbin' about?," Tom asked cheerfully. Apparently, Stuart was continuing to win them over, even off of church property.

"Oh, what else? Paint color," Shannon replied with a wink.

Helen clasped her hands together. "Oh, Abby," she said. "I do hope you like the color we painted this room."

Abby nodded, swallowing past the huge lump in her throat. Her father, the great needs here, the mess of ministry... "It's perfect."

"Oh, good!," Helen said. "Shannon painted her salon walls bright red and thought about doing the same here until I reeled her in. Shannon, what was that color called?"

"Fire engine mystique," she replied, then to Abby, "which was a pretty lame name in my opinion, but the paint looked good once it was all up and dry."

Helen laughed. "Yes! Fire engine whatever, and it was *beautiful*! I started regretting that we hadn't done the same here afterwards, but I think I was right about it needing to be 'neutral' and all."

Tom put his hand on her shoulder affectionately. "Well, we need to be getting these two back to the church. They probably want a few minutes to talk by themselves, I imagine."

And how. Abby managed a smile as she and Stu followed the trio out of the lovely, little home, her mind reeling.

Stu

"How are you feeling?," Stu asked, as he held her hand and walked beside her, after they had waved goodbye to the committee.

"I'm feeling a lot," she said, very simply as he opened the passenger door of the car for her.

"Let's go over to the next town and talk, okay?," he asked, knowing even as he said it that if they came here? They would, literally, have to go over to the next town to get any privacy, likely.

Abby nodded wordlessly as he shut the door behind her and got into the driver's seat himself.

As they drove, Stu let his mind sort through all he'd heard and witnessed.

A church. A church with real problems. A church with real hurts. A church in need of Christ. A church in need of hearing Biblical teaching, week after week, not for just a season but for the long-term.

He'd imagined himself in just such a place. Not a trendy place like Sean's, not a huge church like his grandfather's... but something small, where he could learn alongside the congregation, could grow into this position, and could bring to them what he had, what they needed – clear Biblical teaching and stability, someone who could address the problem frankly, and could work with a whole assortment of people so very different from him.

The problems gave him pause, of course, and the history of pastors who had likely been run off made him question his conclusion, the conclusion that even now he knew as certainty.

He was the man for this church.

He glanced over at Abby, not at all surprised to see that she wore a shell-shocked expression.

"Abby," he murmured, "what are you thinking?"

"I'm thinking," she said, softly, "about my dad."

Stu had thought about him more than once that morning, too. He respected his father-in-law, of course, for having raised a daughter who knew Scripture like she did, who valued the things of God like she did, and for being compassionate and kind like she was.

Beyond that, though, Stu saw little life or passion for anything in the man. He had often wished for the opportunity to have known him long before the end of his ministry, back before he was a man bereft of any goodwill towards God or the people of God, hurt and pained from all that had been done as he watched helplessly from the pulpit.

"What about your dad?," Stu asked, reaching over for her hand.

"Just that... hurt people hurt people, don't they?," she said, swallowing, taking his hand in her own. "I don't know that I can do this, Stu."

He took a small breath. "Well, we're not walking into anything until we're certain. And until we can walk into it together."

She glanced over at him. "It's every bit as bad as it sounds... and then some likely. What they've been through, what they've done to pastors in the meantime. But, even still.... I heard Shannon talking about the hope that she has, the needs, the desire to really see something good of this, and I'm making excuses for them, saying that they only hurt people because along the line they got hurt. Am I crazy?"

"No," he smiled. "You're just thinking like… a pastor's wife, likely."

And as the next town came into view, he took a breath, looking forward to what would come next.

Abby

Okay. So maybe they *would* come back here.

The longer she talked to Stu over dinner that night, in the next town, the more she heard his heart, the more her mind replayed all that they had heard and seen and suspected, the more her heart softened towards the idea.

It was crazy. Absolutely crazy. And she didn't *want* this.

But she could try. And she could pray and hope that her heart would keep turning towards this, if this is what God had for Stu.

She would do anything for Stu. She could do even this.

She was convinced, finally, as they made their way back to the church that night, that it might work out after all.

When they arrived again, hand in hand, they were surprised to find that they weren't the first to the church. They came in through the office, then paused when they heard raised voices in the fellowship hall.

There was arguing. Not about the Huntingtons… but about all that might keep them from coming. Abby could hear Shannon yelling at Horace, Tom yelling at Merle, Helen crying softly, and no one listening to anyone. If these people were representatives of the entire church… then the church was a mess.

Worse than they thought.

Abby had known it before, but she had believed it would be okay. In her desire to see Stu where he thought he should be, she had begun to tentatively believe the best about this church, about church in general.

What a mistake that had been.

As the voices continued to rise, Abby was taken back to the past, when the angry voices were directed towards the strongest man she had known up until then. He was no longer strong.

And there was no way these people were going to do the same to Stuart. To them.

To her.

Stuart listened from outside as they argued, as Abby began to cry.

"Hey," he whispered, drawing her close and walking her back out to the car.

Without a word to one another, they got in, shut the doors, and looked at one another.

"What's wrong?," he asked.

She rolled her eyes.

"Okay, okay," he said. "That, in there – that's what's wrong. But you. Abby. Not even thirty minutes ago, you were onboard, *knowing* that this was probably part of it. The arguing, the conflict, the hurts… hurt people hurt people, you said, and –"

"I can't do this, Stu," she cried. "I thought, you know, when I was talking with Shannon, when we were seeing needs, when we were seeing how God might use you to change eternity here for these people, to lead them to be more like Christ… I thought I could. But this? The yelling, the fighting? I'd sooner die than go through this again. Or, geez, go to Sean's church instead! Do you see that, Stu? That this place? Is a preacher-killing place? And that we'd be better off, if you're intent on doing this, that we'd be better off somewhere like Hope Church, where they aren't completely dysfunctional."

Stu said nothing for a moment. "What if it... isn't as bad as it seems?"

"Seriously?," she gasped. "You can't see what's happening?"

He shook his head. "I didn't say that. I'm just sensing that maybe, quite possibly..." He looked back at the church, biting his lip. "I want to go where God is calling us."

"He's *not* calling us *here*," she hissed. "And He's *not* calling us into ministry." She let out a long breath.

And she made her decision. With or without him.

"I've played at this long enough, Stu. Almost long enough that I got swept up in it and convinced myself. So praise God that we got to see the fight tonight to help me see the light."

Stu watched her for a moment. "How can we be hearing two entirely different things?"

"I don't know," she managed between gritted teeth, thinking only, *I'm right, and YOU are WRONG.*

"Well," he sighed. "We still have an evening service. And then a vote, likely."

"After which you can tell them we're not coming," she laughed bitterly. "Or you can save your breath and tell them right now, before they even expect you to get up and preach."

They stared at one another, wordlessly communicating the ins and outs of a conflict that would likely not be resolved no matter how long they sat in the car, that would only be resolved if he did what she was telling him to do, and –

"We're doing the service," he said, leaving no room for her to argue.

And with that, he left her in the car and walked back into the big middle of the nightmare.

CHAPTER SIX

Stu

Well, no more of this.

Stu very nearly smiled as he recalled that night in the dorm years ago with a very young Abby. He'd just said what he thought, with nothing to lose, pointing out where she was veering towards a dangerous road because he genuinely felt responsible for her.

And look how that had turned out. She was married to him, in love with him... sitting out in his car even now, furious with him.

But they were more than one angry night. Stu was confident of it, even as he walked his way to the fellowship hall, knowing that the same Stuart Huntington who said what he was thinking, offering a timely rebuke when it was needed, was certainly needed here.

And if they rebuffed him? Well, he had nothing to lose. But he was more certain that he had everything to gain and that this would be his first move as their pastor.

All eyes shot to him as he stepped through the doors. He paused for a moment, regarding all of them carefully, knowing just the words to say, just the voice to use, and just the way to communicate with them.

He'd spent his life winning people over. He'd spent his life using words. And he would do it here.

"What seems to be the problem?," he asked calmly, looking back and forth between them all.

Horace sighed. "Oh, nothing."

Shannon blew out a breath at this. "Please."

"You know, Shannon," Horace began again, raising his voice, "a lot of our problems here would be solved if you would just –"

"I told her the truth!," Shannon yelled. "Don't you think it's better for the two of them to know the truth coming in here, about the church split, than –"

"It wasn't a church split!," Tom interjected, anger in his voice. "It wasn't that! It was –"

"It destroyed this church," Merle put in, pounding his hand on the table. "And it –"

"Hold up," Stu said, in a calm voice that quelled the rising storm coming up again in the fellowship hall. "Just... hold on."

And he could sense, as he often did with people, that his words, his simple words, were persuasive enough to calm the worst of emotions, the most outlandish reactions, the greatest conflicts... and they did, here in this room.

"I think," Stu said, as they all watched him, "that there are some really big problems at this church."

Understatement of the year, likely, he thought as he watched their faces.

"Not unlike a lot of churches," Helen said softly.

"No," Stuart said, shaking his head. "Worse than most churches, I think. And I'm not going to blow sunshine in your faces or pretend that everything is okay. Or, worse yet, pretend that I don't know just exactly what's going on here. You people – you here in this room and all of you outside of this room in the church building – have lost sight of who Christ is. Or, quite possibly have never known Him for who He is. And quite honestly, there isn't a sane man who would walk into this situation to lead you to a thriving, growing congregation when it's clear that none of you can resolve your own personal heart issues enough to get to that point."

They all stared at him as he stared right back.

"That said," he said, "I want to ask you all to shut your mouths, stop talking about who has killed this church, and start listening to what Christ has to say, in Scripture, about your own depravity. If we can start there? Maybe we can get somewhere."

That was Stu. Saying what he thought, with nothing to lose.

And with everything to gain, as even then, even still, his words began to sow peace in hearts, the reaping of which he might one day see himself as pastor of this wounded, weary flock.

Abby

Reverend and Mrs. Stuart Huntington. Rev. and Mrs…

It was very nearly all Abby could think as she walked back into the mess. The mess that was calling itself a church, pulling Stu into their midst with gnarled, angry, needful embraces. Embraces that would likely turn and toss him out before they could even unpack at the parsonage.

She was going in anyway. But she was only going in there for Stu. No one else. Just Stu. She'd gone into the restroom at the church to throw some water on her face, to hide the tears, seething at Stu even as she did this for him, feeling heartbroken all at the same time over the fact that he hadn't come back to find her. As she'd been standing there, redoing her makeup, Shannon had walked in, wiping her eyes as well.

"Hey," she said, smiling.

"Hey," Abby murmured, steeling herself against any good emotions or kindred feelings she would be tempted to have towards this woman. She wouldn't let herself be pulled back in, not into this mess, not into this crazy, horrific nightmare called pastoral ministry, and –

As she was reaching for the tube of mascara she'd packed earlier that morning, she inadvertently knocked her purse to the floor, where the contents spilled out on the linoleum and began rolling around.

"Here, let me help you," Shannon said.

"Thanks," Abby managed. "My head's just all over the place."

"Lots to think on," Shannon agreed. "It's a big move, coming out here, changing up your life entirely."

She had no clue just what a big deal it was, as she continued passing makeup and tissues over to Abby, pausing for just a moment as her hand hesitated over the little blue pack.

"Wouldn't want to forget these," she said, smiling up at Abby as she put the pills back in her purse for her.

And Abby felt her heart seize with great alarm. She *had* forgotten them. Oh, good grief. How long had it been since...

Knowing that Shannon watched and honestly not caring, Abby checked the date on the prescription card on the front. August. She was... two months off the pill.

Two. Months.

In the insanity that had accompanied Stu's enigmatic calling, Abby had simply gotten out of the habit – a habit that was already spotty, unfortunately – and stopped taking the pills altogether. How long had they been hidden at the bottom of her purse?

Two months, at least, given the nearly full pack.

More alarming than this, though, was the fact that she couldn't remember if she'd even had a period since then.

Shannon mistook her alarm for nerves regarding the decision ahead of them and told her, reassuringly, "It's all really going to be okay, Abby."

Abby simply nodded in response.

It was more of the same, as he stood to preach, as he shared the very same things, and as the congregation left, visibly affected, visibly moved, and visibly convicted about where they stood with Christ as individuals, as a congregation….as a church body.

He had nothing to lose. And the freedom this afforded him was the very freedom that led him to say the things that they needed to hear.

And they told him, before he and Abby could leave, that he was the man for their church.

No doubts. Certainty. And they were waiting for him to come back, to bring them to a place of true worship and sincerity of faith, and speak words of healing and restoration over their community.

Abby wanted no part of it. She thought on these things as she and Stu drove away, silence stretching between them.

"I know you're angry," he said, quite simply.

Angry. Confused. Terrified.

And pregnant. Most likely pregnant, and my, wouldn't that complicate everything.

"I'm not angry, Stu," she said.

"You've not said one word to me since we left the church," he said.

"You haven't said one word to *me*, Stu," she bit back.

"That's really childish, Abby," he muttered.

She wanted to laugh out loud at the ill-timed word "childish," but she kept her own mounting hysteria in check, as she blurted out, "I'm just really worn out, Stu. Have been for a while. And I'd like to table this discussion you're intent on having until tomorrow. Can we do that? Can we wait until tomorrow?"

He glanced over at her, surprised by her sudden stream of words. "If that would help you to have a clearer mind, then –"

"Can you stop here?," she asked, pointing to the gas station up ahead. "I've got to use the restroom." *And buy a pregnancy test. And take the stupid test so that I don't spend another second wondering if –*

"Yeah, I need to put gas in the car anyway," he said.

Before he could even take the key out of the ignition, right as he turned to look at her, she bolted from the car. She found what she needed on the dusty shelves of the convenience store quickly enough, paid the ridiculous amount they were charging for it, and was in the restroom, three minutes later, holding the completed test in her hand and waiting for her future to be revealed. Just as she was beginning to wonder if the time of day the sample was taken would make a difference in the accuracy, two lines appeared. Fumbling with the box, she gasped to see what was written there.

Pregnant.

Well.

She threw all the evidence away, washed her hands, and wandered out of the restroom in a haze. Stu had come in as well by then, and he walked up to her, concern on his face.

"You okay?," he murmured, even as she stared at him.

"I'm fine," she lied. "Just fine."

Stu

They got back just in time for him to go back to work.

Back at the shipping facility, working all night after a long and emotionally draining day.

But unlike all the days spent at the political party office, selling his very soul for a pittance, Stu felt energized and alive after the day they'd had.

There was Abby, of course, whose silence on the drive home had been understandable. Sean's words about how she could be holding them back came to him again and again, and he couldn't help, in the deepest part of his heart, to resent her for her tight-lipped, angry expression as they drove away. He resented her father for making her this way, resented the church of the past for making her like this, and resented her most of all for allowing it to happen.

It showed a complete lack of faith.

And her actions, her behavior as of late, showed a complete lack of sanity, honestly. She'd been really emotional, ever since he'd started seminary, and while he could understand it in part, the manic-depressive heights and depths she soared and plunged from were extreme, to say the least.

She'd stormed into the apartment and gotten ready for bed, never even asking him about work, about what they'd just been through, about when they could talk.

He'd stared at her, even as she plopped into their bed, her back to him, as he got ready. How different this was from the majority of nights, when she'd face him, talk to him, tell him she'd miss him, threaten to make him late to work by pulling him into bed with her and distracting him from the clock that demanded his attention and —

But not tonight. No, tonight it was her back. Even as he grabbed his keys, prepared to leave, she didn't turn to face him. So, he crawled in next to her, nuzzled her neck, and said, "Aren't you even going to kiss me goodbye?"

He could feel her blow out an exasperated breath at this. Then, she turned around to face him, put her hands to his face, and gave him the most passionate kiss he'd ever been given.

Passionately angry, that is.

She broke away from him, gave him a tight, forced smile, and spat out, "There. Darling." Before he could comment or respond, she flopped right back over, her back to him again.

It couldn't be helped. Not tonight, at least. But there would be the next morning. And they would work this out.

Surely.

Abby

Stu usually got home at five in the morning. Abby was up earlier than that, though. Sick.

Not physically, of course. No, she'd managed to avoid that first sign of pregnancy without even knowing that she'd dodged the bullet. The sickness that she battled that morning was a racing mind, full of too many questions and no answers, apprehension, worry, and memories, sad and terrifying memories.

She called in sick for the first time in her life, knowing that she would be no good at school until there was some sort of resolution with Stu.

She loved him. And she would resolve this. Because he wouldn't keep on with this crazy plan if he could see, if he could really see, what it was doing to her.

She made him a huge breakfast, prepared to have this talk with him.

When he came home, she could see the exhaustion in his face, the wariness in his eyes as he looked at her. She cursed the hormones that brought tears to her own eyes, the very same hormones that had been making everything so much more emotional these past two months.

"Hey," he said softly.

"Hey," she responded back. And she walked to him, reached up for his face, whispered "come here," and kissed him. Because no matter what came next, even still, she loved Stu.

She hated what he was doing, but she loved him.

"Abby," he murmured, pulling her close. "Are we okay? Are you okay?"

"I'm just fine," she sighed. "Called the school today, told them that I wasn't coming in, though. Because we've got to work this out."

He nodded. "Yeah. Eat first, then talk, hmm?"

"Yeah," she agreed.

And they ate in silence, until Stu was nearly done, until she could stand it no longer. "I can't do this," she said.

"Can't do what?," he asked.

"I can't be around those people. I can't live there. They're... vicious. And mean. And they'll eat you alive, Stu."

He sighed. "They will do no such thing, Abby."

"They have no concern for Christ and certainly less for you. I want absolutely nothing to do with them."

"You would think," he said, calmly, patiently, "that you'd be a little more gracious and charitable about these things, having grown up in ministry yourself." He shot her a look that held no grace or charity either one. Just frustration and exhaustion, likely from dealing with her mood swings.

Well, he could deal.

"You would think that, wouldn't you, Stu?," she hissed. "Godly, PK Abby, lying herself out before the masses of pagan pew sitters, just begging them to walk all over me."

"Good grief, Abby –"

"You are *always* like this, Stu!," she yelled at him. "You come in with *your* plans, *your* ideas, and *your* way of thinking and just expect that everyone else will line up according to *you*. From the first moment I met you, you were telling me what I was doing wrong and how I should get right like you. And now, it's more of the same."

He gave her an even look. "I'm not asking you to do anything," he said, "other than staying open to the very real possibility that –"

"The very real possibility that everything is going to be in complete upheaval? I mean, apart from the church and what they'll likely do to us, have you even stopped and thought about *my* career? *My* job? Because I can't keep teaching where I'm at if I'm following you out to the middle of nowheresville."

"You'll get a job there," he said, as if she was stupid for not making the logical connection with him. "You'll go and get a job there, and –"

"Again, telling me what I should do," she seethed at him.

He shook his head. "I'm not telling you what to do. I'm giving you logical answers to the questions you're asking. But, Abby, half of the questions you're asking are completely *illogical*. You talk about ministry as though they're out to get us. That's not the way it works. A normal, healthy, growing church will –"

"Still not get it right every time!," she continued, shocked to hear herself now screeching at him. "And when they hurt us, I should feel glad about it, right? I should thank them for hurting me so as to make me holy, right? I'll put on my freakin' crown and dance all around, right, Stu?"

"Sometimes it's not about feelings," he said. "It's not about how *you* feel. Sometimes it's about the simple truth of something. God is not who He is because you feel He should be a certain way. And this church is not going to be the way it is because you feel it should be a certain way. You're letting every bit of emotion and feeling you have sweep you away to these illogical places, and it –"

"I would go there, for you, Stu, but geez! Have you even thought through what they're –"

"Don't go anywhere in ministry for *me*, Abby," he said, looking at her. "It will get you nowhere because I'm going to let you down. You should do this because God is calling you to it."

Oh, and God most certainly wouldn't *dare* to do that. Not knowing how she felt, how she couldn't trust even God Himself to protect Stuart from this church, and –

"These people are going to ruin you," she said. "Just like people just like them ruined my dad."

"These people," he said, heatedly, "haven't done a *thing* to you, Abby. To me either! And you're acting like you're so much better than they are –"

"I'm not better than them," she hissed. And that was when she couldn't argue his points... so she went for the hurt. "But I have my misgivings about following *you* into this kind of mess, Stu. I mean, really."

He regarded her with confusion. "And by that you mean... what, exactly?"

"Forgive me," she said, "for not being nearly as holy as you are about the whole mess."

"I'm not being holy," he said. "I'm only trying to do the right thing. And to continue on, ignoring God's call for our lives –"

"*Your* life," she swore.

He took a breath. "Ignoring God's call, for either of us, would be the wrong thing to do."

And she knew it was wrong, but she couldn't keep herself from saying it, knowing that it would wound him, would make him question his own judgment, his very own qualification for doing what he was so intent on doing to them. "And after all the wrong things you've done, I suppose that makes you the expert, huh? Think the church will still want you if they knew half the stuff you've done?"

As much as her words cut him, they didn't hurt him nearly as much as they hurt her. No sooner were they out of her mouth than she was wishing them back, knowing that she'd broken a promise, to never bring his past up again, to forgive him as Christ had forgiven him...

… way to go, Abby.

And yet even still, she couldn't keep herself from standing firm and holding back an apology.

"You said," Stu began softly, "that you'd never bring that up again."

"Well, we said a lot of things, didn't we, Stuart?"

He said nothing for a moment. "I think you're so poisoned by what happened to your dad that you aren't even thinking clearly. And I'm not going to hold it against you. Because I love you, Abby."

"How very charitable of you," she sniped.

"You're letting your dad's hurts stand in the way of what God is doing now. You're letting the people who hurt him pull you away from what God wants you to do."

"Do you know what they did?," she said, tears running down her face. "Do you know how they twisted everything he said, how they froze him out of their social circles, how they yelled at us, how they made our lives absolutely miserable? Do you know how they took my father, who loved Jesus and only wanted to serve Him, and made him despise the church? Do you know, Stu?"

Stu took a breath. "I'm sorry that it happened. But it doesn't happen to everyone. And we're better equipped than most, knowing what could happen, worst case scenario. Or best case scenario, like Sean and Jennie –"

"*Please!*," she screeched, stomping her feet like a child. "Don't talk about *Jennie!*"

"Real mature, Abby," he said.

She flashed him a look of seething rage, and he responded with, "Forget Jennie, then. Best case scenario, I could be like my grandfather, persevering in ministry at the same thriving church for all those decades. And my grandmother, a pastor's daughter herself, right by his side, just like the kind of pastor's wife you would be, Abby –"

"I don't want to be a pastor's wife!," she yelled. Silence as they stared at each other. "I don't want any part of it, Stu! I don't want to be married to a pastor!"

He didn't say anything for a moment. Then, quietly, "But you're married to me."

And she said the words that she wouldn't be able to take back. The words she very sincerely meant right then and there. "I don't want to be married to you anymore."

Before Stu could respond, shock and pain in his expression, Abby took her keys into her hand and stormed out of the apartment.

CHAPTER SEVEN

Abby

So. Where does a pregnant pastor's wife go when she's angry at the world?

Correction, Abby reminded herself, as she swiped at her eyes and the tears that wouldn't stop. She wasn't a pastor's wife. And surely Stu would stop this nonsense, because if he didn't, she would...

What? What would she do? Honestly leave him? Walk away from him? As if the pain of that thought, of being apart from Stu, wasn't enough... she was pregnant with his child now. How much did that complicate things?

She continued driving, wondering how it had gotten to this.

It had all started back at the little church. Her father's second pastorate, one that they had been hesitant to go to, given the love they felt for their first church. But the call came, her parents felt it was God's will for them, and they moved to the new town, the new state, and their new lives, ready to see what He was going to do with them.

For the first three years, things were wonderful. There were problems, of course, but that was true of any church. It wasn't until the association of churches joined together with plans to fund a mission church in an unreached part of the state that... well, that things got bad.

There was talk of members being deceived, of funds being mis-allocated, of decisions being made apart from the rules of church bylaws and expectations. And as all of these things combined to create a firestorm of accusations and conflicts, the true hearts of many church members became evident.

Wolves among the sheep, Abby knew. But at fourteen, it's one thing to know the Scripture that you've taught to tiny children and trusted as ultimate truth and quite another to watch as mean, cruel people wrongly and efficiently tear down the godliest man you've ever known.

Abby remembered many tense moments from business meetings, all out yelling in the church offices, and snubs around town from people who had claimed to love them. She remembered how worn out her father seemed all the time, how he had to go on blood pressure medication, and how he yelled at his own children from time to time, because there was just no way to stop once he started. She remembered how her mother, her precious, calm, godly mother, had gotten a call from a deacon's wife on the phone one afternoon, how she had stood there being berated and belittled for nearly fifteen minutes, and how she hung up the phone and cried.

"She was my friend, Abby," she sobbed. "My only friend."

Abby felt physically sick at the remembrance. Stu thought that the worst part of the entire fiasco had been her father. The anger, the depression, the end of his faith – it had been catastrophic for a fourteen year old girl.

But the worst... the worst was her mother. Crying in the kitchen. Then, throwing the phone to the floor and sobbing because there was nothing she could do.

Her mother had spent the better part of that horrific year watching the conflict unfold. She'd sat by and watched it, unable to say anything, because the pastor's wife couldn't say a thing. She had to be as blameless as her husband, standing by him and taking what was dealt to him. But she couldn't speak to it, couldn't defend herself, because in doing so, she would become part of the problem.

She would have just become another problem for the pastor to fix.

So, she had to stay silent, even as the church destroyed everything and everyone around her.

It was a lonely place to be. And a hopeless one, apart from the hope of Christ, which was but a dim hope at times in the sad little parsonage, where they had trouble seeing anything but the unredeemed.

Abby would *not* become *that*.

Stu couldn't make her do it. He wouldn't dream of asking her if he knew what it was really like.

She was driving with no destination when her phone buzzed. Certain that it was Stu, calling to tell her to come home so they could talk, she picked it up, eager to hear him say that they would work this out, that they, the two of them, were more important than anyone else –

"Abs?"

Not Stu. Not the voice she wanted to hear.

But Grant. Comforting. Familiar. Even still.

"Hey, Grant," she said, still sniffling.

"Hey, do you have any idea where Seth and Rachel are?," he asked, tension in his voice. "I've been trying both of their cell phones for the past hour, and neither one of them is picking up."

"Probably both on their way to work," she managed around her tears.

"Keep trying."

He sighed. "Well, I plan on it. There's a building that just came up for lease, and I'm telling you, Abs, it's perfect for the restaurant, and I wanted them to..." He trailed off. "Abs, are you crying?"

She was. She had been. And she probably would be for a good, long while.

"Yeah," she sobbed. "A little."

"Sweetheart," he said, the endearment falling from his lips so sincerely and easily, "are you okay?"

"No," she cried. "I'm not."

Only silence for a moment, as she heard Grant take a deep breath. "Is it Stu? Did Stu do something wrong?"

And Stu? Had done nothing wrong. Nothing that anyone else would see as wrong.

Except Grant. Maybe Grant. Because during that summer of strawberry, she had told him what it was like, to be shunned from their church, for their lives to be turned upside down...

... maybe he would get it.

"Oh, it's just... he just wants to be a pastor," she said.

"Geez, Abs," he sighed. "I can see why you'd be upset."

Of course, he would. Grant knew her. Grant understood. Grant had always been a great listener. Grant had always been there.

And for a brief moment, Abby wondered what it would have been like had it been Grant she'd reconnected with that fall, so many years ago, instead of Stuart. She would find herself in a precarious spot now with the restaurant, of course, but surely it would be better than the pastorate. It would be Grant she'd be walking this road with, Grant who would come home happy every night, Grant who would understand her past, Grant who would be there for her future, Grant who would be the father of the child she was carrying –

And that was too far. It was taking it too far. And Abby knew it, even as Grant said, "Abs, come to the apartment. We can talk. I'll fix you something to eat. You don't need to keep driving if you're upset."

She shouldn't. She wouldn't. Even as she opened her mouth to tell him that she couldn't, her phone beeped at her again.

"Grant, I've got another call," she stammered, clicking to the next call, shutting the door behind her. Please be Stu, she prayed silently. Oh, God, if You're listening, please let it be Stu –

"ABS!," Rachel shrieked in her ear.

Not Stu. So not Stu. "Hey," Abby offered, sighing.

"Oh, my, *gosh*, Abs!," Rachel continued, not discerning any sadness in her friend's voice. "He did it! He finally did it! Seth freakin' *kissed* me! Totally *made out* with me!"

And this little tidbit was distracting enough that Abby stopped crying, stopped thinking back to the troubling conversation with Grant… but didn't stop thinking of Stu, wondering if he was trying to call her.

"This isn't a great time, Rachel," she said, eager to try calling him herself. "I'll call you back later."

And as she hung up the phone, before she could dial his number, she was surprised to see where she had driven herself.

Stu

His wife was going to leave him.

Abby... she didn't want him anymore.

Stu wasn't sure how to handle what had happened. Had he neglected the most important institution – marriage – for the love of another – the church? How would he be fit to lead a church if he couldn't lead his family?

How would he be fit to live without Abby?

He called Seth. He needed Seth to pray. And the idiot couldn't even manage that over the phone, giving short, clipped answers, guilt in his voice, finally just saying that he'd be over in a minute.

He must have sped the whole way over because he arrived, literally, within minutes of hanging up.

"Hey," Stu said, opening up the door, ready to tell Seth all that needed to be prayed for –

"Oh, crap," Seth said as a hello. "Crap, crap, crap!"

So, he knew. He must have known about Abby, about Stu's problem, about the demise of his marriage –

"I kissed Rachel, man," Seth practically whispered.

"What?," Stu asked, momentarily diverted from his own problem.

"I kissed Rachel!," he hissed. "She came at me, and I kissed her!"

Stu sighed. "As much as I would enjoy saying I told you so, I really have bigger problems right now."

"No way you could have bigger problems," Seth shook his head. "I kissed her. And she kissed me. And...well, my hands were everywhere, Stu! And... other parts of me were about to be everywhere as well! I was ripping off my clothes as fast as I could, and... well, she was actually doing most of that herself, and I –"

"Where exactly was all of this happening?"

"Her house!"

"Was Grant there?"

Seth shot him a look. "Do you think I would have let his sister undress me had he been there, man?!"

Stu frowned. "Crap, Seth. Why were you even there, alone with her–"

"Because I'm an idiot," Seth groaned. "Just an absolute idiot."

Stu sighed. "Well, yeah."

"Oh, geez, am I glad you called when you did!," Seth said, actually reaching out and embracing his brother. "Of course, my mind already went all the places my body wanted to go, but, Stu, you saved me. You saved me! With that call! How did you know I needed you to call, right then –"

"I didn't, you idiot," Stu said. "I called because for once, *I* needed *you*."

Seth said nothing for a moment. "Isn't that totally God? On the one morning you did, I was over there totally prepared to... well, you know, but He allowed some calamity in your life so you'd pick up your phone, call me, and get me to stop –"

"Shut up. Shut up, shut up, shut up!," Stu spat out. "Right now, I don't want to talk about that. I'm really in trouble, Seth. Abby... she..." And he lowered his head to his hands and let out a discouraged breath.

"What?," Seth said, softly. "What's wrong with Abby?"

"I think she's going to leave me."

"No," Seth managed after a moment of silence. "She wouldn't... she loves you. The two of you are perfect together."

"Well, we were, but... this whole seminary and church thing... she's just freaking out on me. And she told me she doesn't..." He looked up at Seth. "She doesn't want to be married to me anymore."

Seth stared at him. "Was it that bad at the church this weekend?"

Stu had told him all about it before the fact, had known Seth would be praying, and had every intention of calling him with an update before the explosion this morning.

"It wasn't bad. It was... great. I know I'm the man for the job, but Abby just isn't on board, and –"

"Stu," Seth interjected, "if your wife isn't on board, then maybe you aren't the man for the job."

Stu watched him for a moment. "No, you don't understand. These people are in conflict and are hurting and are really needing someone to come in and take charge and –"

"Conflict? Sounds like a really great place," Seth murmured.

Stu frowned. "It doesn't matter what it sounds like. If God's calling me there, then it's the right place. And I saw progress. Even just this one weekend."

"You've only known these people one weekend, man," Seth said. "And you've known Abby for three years. And she's your wife. Your wife."

"I know that," Stu said irritably.

"Did you talk to her about it, listen to how she felt?"

"Well, yeah, I..." He had. He had listened. He had heard her. And he had gone on and done what they were supposed to do.

Without her. He left her crying in the car.

"Crap," he sighed.

"I'm not making excuses for Abby," Seth said. "I mean, I don't even know the whole story. But I can't see that God would call you somewhere that He wouldn't... well, that He wouldn't be calling Abby as well."

And Stu could see his fault in this, could see Abby's reservation... but still, even still, wouldn't they be called to the same thing?

"What if she's not listening to God, though?," Stu murmured.

Seth shrugged. "You love her anyway. You stay with her. You do what keeps you one with Abby. Because a church? A job? God's never going to call you to something that destroys what He's already established. And you and Abby, in marriage? He established that."

Stu frowned, then felt his face relax as he sighed. "How did you get to be so smart?"

Seth rolled his eyes. "Oh, I'm not smart. Not even thirty minutes ago, I was showing the depth of my stupidity, all over my best friend's kid sister, and... crap, man."

"Crap, indeed," Stu nodded. "For both of us."

"Well, hey, your problem can be fixed, right now." Seth put his hand to his brother's back. "I'll pray, Stu. Let's pray. For Abby."

Abby

Abby found herself at Jennie and Sean's, uncertain that this was the place to find her answers. But Jennie literally wrote the book on young, godly marriage, particularly young, godly marriage to a man called to

144

ministry.

Surely Jennie could help. Surely Jennie would help talk some sense into her. Surely Jennie would be a sympathetic ear. Surely Jennie –

-- wasn't standing in the kitchen of her dream home, sobbing in Scott's arms.

Wait a minute. Wrong Huntington brother. *Really* wrong Huntington brother. Abby looked away for a second, then back, sure her vision would correct itself, and that Jennie would be clinging to Sean, and –

But there she was, even still, sobbing in their brother-in-law's arms as he looked around like a deer in someone's headlights, patting her on the back as she held onto him.

"There, there," he said, almost mechanically, as his blank expression turned Abby's direction and he continued patting Jennie on the back.

"And you, Scott," she sobbed, "are a blessing. A real, real blessing! And every word I've said against you, in my sin and my irritation and my flesh – I take it back! Because I can see Jesus in you, Scott, in who He's going to make you, in who you're going to be in Him, and –"

"Well," he sighed, "that's a lot to conclude after watching me fix a broken showerhead. But I appreciate it, Jennie."

"Please don't hold my past misbehavior against me, Scott," she sobbed. "I haven't been fair to you, and –"

"You've been more than fair," he said. "You've been honest. And I've never thought badly of you because of it."

"Really?"

He shrugged. "Well, not too badly." Before she could fall in his arms again, he said, "Hey, why don't you go check it out?"

"Okay," sniffed. "Hey, Ab-by." Singsong voice. Even still.

She went on, sniffling as she did.

Scott turned to Abby. "Did Sean call you, too?"

"No," Abby shook her head. "What's going on?"

"Jennie is a cup and a half of crazy," he said simply. "Broken showerhead this morning. Sean called Dad, and because Dad doesn't work at the butt crack of dawn these days because – oh, yeah – he has *me* for that, he called me to have me come and fix it." A pause. "You would think Sean would know a few things about basic home maintenance just by having Dad's genes, but I swear, the man has screwed up so many things in this house with his ineptitude. As soon as I took care of the shower, I started working on everything else, and Jennie's been all over me, dripping with gratitude." He sighed. "I need a drink."

"This early in the morning?"

"Oh, yeah," he said, picking up his tools. "You gonna talk her off the ledge? The boys are already up and covered in their breakfast. I'm not sure that Jennie –"

"*It works! Scott, you're a saint!*," Jennie yelled from the bathroom.

"Yeah," he whispered to Abby. "Cup and a half of crazy." Then, raising his voice, "Check out the lights in your closets, Jennie!"

"Fixed that, too, huh?," Abby asked.

"Yeah," he said, looking at his watch. "You know, the longer I stay around here the more likely it is that the even crazier woman at home waiting on me will give up and leave. Which I'm hoping she will after last night."

"There's a woman waiting for you?"

"Yeah. Some girl named..." Scott blinked at her for a second. "Misty?

Or… Crystal?" He shrugged. "I don't remember her name, frankly. It was a weird night, honestly, and she's crazier than Jennie, so I won't *need* to remember her name, since it ain't ever happenin' again –"

"Geez," Abby sighed, "are you sure you're related to Stu? Or *any* of your brothers?"

He shrugged again. "I gotta be me, Abby." Then, an idea hit him. "Hey, if you called over to my place and went all psycho-crazy on her when she answers the phone, like you're my other woman or something –"

"Scott –"

"No, seriously, it would help me out," he said. "Charity, Abby. For your brother-in-law. For your family." He nodded solemnly. "To make it up to Stu."

"Who said I have anything to make up to Stu?," she asked, gaping at him, thinking back to her thoughts on Grant.

"Just a random shot in the dark guess," he said, "that's totally apt, apparently, judging by that look on your face."

"And how would cleaning up your mess be making up anything to Stu?," she asked.

"Because you're extending this kindness to his favorite brother."

"You're not his –"

He held out the phone. "Go on, now. Deranged, psycho, half a cup of crazy, at least –"

She groaned and took his phone. A few seconds passed before a woman (who still sounded half asleep) answered. "Hello?"

Abby took a deep breath, as Scott motioned her on.

"Who is this?!," she spat out.

A pause. "Who is *this*?"

"Is Scott there?!," Abby rolled her eyes. "Put Scott on the line!"

"Scott's not here….who is this?"

"His *wife*," she said. "I am his *wife*. And that cheating loser has done it again! Girl, you better get yourself checked out because my man? Is a skank! A total *skank*!"

Scott made a face… then gave her a thumbs up.

"*What*?!"

"Yeah, I'm the skank's wife," Abby continued on, imagining for a brief moment just how mean and nasty she would get if this woman was messing around with Stu. "I'm on my way home right now, and I swear, if you're still in my bed when I get there, I will –"

The woman hung up on her. Abby handed the phone back to Scott with a frown.

"Well," he sighed, "I'm a little offended by the whole skank comment, but since you got the job done? I'll overlook it. Thank you, Abby. You and Jennie are both crazy in your own special ways. Raging psycho pastors' wives and all –"

"I'm not a pastor's wife," Abby sighed.

"Not yet," he said. "But you *are* my new favorite sister-in-law. And you can be my wingman the next time I go out. Playing my crazy wife whenever I need to scare off unstable women."

"I'll pass," she said.

"*Scott*!," Jennie yelled from across the house. "Do you think you have time to look at –"

"I'm out of here," he muttered, kissing Abby on the cheek just before he slipped out.

"Scott, there's a problem with the –"

She stopped short, just as she came into the kitchen, seeing that he was gone.

"Oh," she murmured sadly. "He's gone. Just like Sean. Does this house repel men, Abby?"

Jennie was a mess. From the top of her unwashed hair to her oversized shirt and sweats and the way she continued, even now, biting her fingernails.

Abby opened her mouth to say something reassuring, when Jennie flopped down in a seat at the table.

"Well, not all men are repelled by this house," she sighed. "Because God knows that Ezra and Nehemiah never, and I mean never, leave this house. Because I can't take them anywhere. Anywhere. They're... monsters. Tiny monsters."

Abby followed her eyes to the living room where the "tiny monsters" were crawling around in their diapers, their shirts crusted over with some soggy type of cereal. And on their heads they wore buckets, which they were beating with the wooden spoons they carried in their hands.

Abby said a quick prayer that twins didn't actually run in the Huntington blood line, despite what they all said and –

"Oh, Abby, I'm pregnant!," Jennie cried, in answer to the question that Abby didn't even ask, regarding the insanity around them. "Oh, sweet Jesus, I am *knocked up*! Again!"

Abby opened her mouth to offer up her congratulations, then stopped short, wondering if she should offer up apologies instead.

Jennie wasn't looking for either, though. Her head shot up from where she had held it in her hands, her eyes red, her tears flowing, her nose running... she was a mess. Oh, wow. Perfect Jennie was a mess.

"And no surprise, right? I mean, Sean doesn't *believe* in birth control," she said. "I mean, have we married into the nuttiest family on earth?! Six kids themselves, and... do you and Stu use birth control?"

Not very well, apparently.

"I know what you're thinking," Jennie continued blubbering.

Abby doubted this very much. "What am I thinking?"

"How," Jennie said, "does a couple have a normal, healthy marriage for five years without a child, right? Without a pregnancy, right? How did we manage to *not* have a child for that long since Sean believes the pill is straight from the depths of hell itself?"

"Well," Abby said, "I just assumed it was a fertility issue. And none of my business, actually —"

"It was totally a fertility issue," Jennie said vehemently. "And by that, I mean I was *in charge* of my fertility. I charted, I temped, I drew such beautiful pictures of my coverline, my baseline, that I was the freakin' Monet of ovulation! And when it was no good, when I knew my body was ready, I faked everything from headaches to rashes to fevers to gas."

Abby frowned.

"Yes, Abby," Jennie said, very seriously. "Sean is a man with only one thing on his mind as soon as he walks through the bedroom door, I swear, but even he, in all of his God-given desire for the wife of his youth wouldn't dream of touching me when I lied and told him I had seriously atomic, hazardous gas and that I'd spent the better part of the evening far—"

"Oh, Jennie," Abby managed, just a bit horrorstruck by this information.

"I'm just saying."

Abby couldn't hide a grin, imagining trendy, hip Sean's reaction to a flatulent wife. "So, you... lied? To get out of —"

"More times than I can count," Jennie said, matter-of-factly. Then, accusing, "Like you haven't done it."

Abby hadn't. Honestly. All those moments of distracting Stu, enjoying him, getting good and knocked up herself, and —

"But your book, Jennie," she said, shaking herself free of those thoughts. "In your book, you tell young wives that —"

"Did you actually read my book, Abby?," Jennie asked, tearing up again. "I gave it to you, thinking that you probably wouldn't read it. Because, you know, you and Savannah hate me."

"We don't hate you," Abby murmured. "I mean, I don't. And Savannah... well, Savannah thinks highly of you. She said once that you have perfect boobs."

After it was out of her mouth, Abby wondered at the entirely inappropriate nature of this comment. Pregnancy brain. Already. Saying what she thought, just like Stu always did, and —

"Savannah thinks my boobs are perfect?," Jennie said, tearing up. "Well, if that's not the sweetest thing ever, Abby! Tell her I said thank you!"

"Sure," Abby said, patting Jennie's hands. "We don't hate you. We never have." They hadn't liked her much, but hate wasn't how they felt.

And honestly? Maybe the hard feelings for Abby, at least, had been part... well, jealousy. The woman was perfect after all.

Even as she sat in the midst of domestic chaos as the twins continuing chattering and screaming intermittently, wiping at her nose with the edge of her shirt.

"But, yeah. I read your book. And it was so good," Abby said. "Really challenging. Very inspiring. I learned a lot." She had. Honestly.

"Really?," Jennie practically whispered.

"Yeah, and I read every, single last word. More than once."

Jennie nodded. "And I meant every word," she cried. "And I still do. I love Sean. I really, really love Sean. But I'm tired. I'm so tired. I spend all day and all night with these little monsters –"

The boys continued beating each other in response.

"And," she took a deep, ragged breath, "I don't ever see Sean. He's always up at the church."

"He's serious about his work," Abby said. "Stu says he's done so well –"

"He has, he has," Jennie sighed, wiping her nose again. "But it owns him. And he's in over his head with this new campus, and... he's just so stressed. And so am I. And my brain is fried. And I can't count, because I totally screwed up the days, and now, we're expecting. Again. I'm as fertile as our crazy mother-in-law!"

Abby reached over and took her hand. "Hey, maybe things will slow down with Sean. Maybe you should... tell him this. He can't know it all, Jennie."

"He can't," she said, "and you're right. But I don't want to be another problem he has to fix. His calling is so big, and I just..." She bit her quivering lip. "I used to *be* someone, Abby. Before I married Sean and had these babies. I mean, I was someone important. I got a job at Grace back when they wouldn't even hire Sean as anything more than an intern. And we all know that even that was all nepotism because of his grandfather, and –"

She clasped a hand to her mouth, apparently shocked that she had voiced her most private thoughts.

"It's okay," Abby murmured.

"No, it's not," Jennie sobbed, "because he's great, even still. And I willingly gave up what I was and who I was to… to be one in Christ with him. And it's been amazing. And it's been greater than I could have planned on my own. But… wow." She lowered her voice to a whisper. "It's so lonely, Abby."

And even though her children were screeching, giving voice to the fact that Jennie never ever had a moment alone to speak of… well, Abby could feel the loneliness.

"But life is more than how I feel," Jennie said. "And I understood that before Sean and I ever met. Life was Christ. Life is Christ. And His truth remains and is… much bigger than how I feel right now." She looked to Abby, starting to cry again. "And I feel really, really crappy right now."

"Me, too," Abby managed, thinking over Stu's words about her feelings, how they had taken precedence over the faith that had been the very thing Stu had loved about her so long ago…

"You know," Jennie said, resolutely, "I just have to trust that God will get us through this rough season and into a better one. He will. I know He will. He has before. Over and over again. And I'm going to be here for Sean, after this season is over. Me, the boys, and this new little one. If I don't lose my mind before then, that is. It's just a season, right? Just a season I have to get through, trusting God, right, Abby? And if I can't even do that, what kind of faith is this that I claim to have anyway, right?"

Right, right, right.

Trusting God. Through seasons.

Abby thought of Stu, of what he was being called to… of what this new season would look like.

And she wanted to be with him, no matter what, trusting what God had.

Finally resting in faith and not in her own self-made security.

"Jennie," she said.

"What?," Jennie asked, taking a deep breath.

"Let me get the boys cleaned up," she said. "And you? You go up to the church and just… I don't know. Surprise Sean. Go have a long talk with him. Take him lunch." A pause. "Seduce him. With those perfect boobs of yours."

Jennie looked down at her oversized shirt critically. "You know, everyone said nursing would take its toll… but I don't see it. I think they're better now than they were. Which is probably at least part of the reason why I find myself, not even six months post-partum, suddenly expecting again."

Abby smiled. "Maybe. Seriously, just go be with him. Tell him you miss him. You two love each other so much. I know he's got to be missing you, too."

Jennie blinked at her. "Really?"

"Yeah, really," Abby said, nodding. "How could he not, right?" She thought on this for a second. "You say that you were somebody before he came along… Jennie, you're somebody now. And you're better than you were because you make Sean better. Imagine what his ministry would be like without you. Imagine what Ezra and Nehemiah and… Hezekiah, or whatever you'll name the next one… well, imagine who they'll be because their mother? *Is* somebody."

And just imagine… who Stu would be, with Abby beside him, confident in Christ, ready to go out in faith with him.

Jennie watched her for an awed moment.

"Why are you being so sweet to me?," she finally asked.

Because you're going to be here for me, just like this, one of these days, Abby thought to herself, looking at perfect Jennie and finally identifying with her.

Sisters in ministry. Young pastors' wives. Tears, snot, and children banging one another on the heads with wooden spoons.

"You're my sister, Jennie," Abby whispered, tears in her own eyes.

And Jennie reached out and embraced her, a flood of tears baptizing them both.

Stu

She called him. Abby called him.

He was functioning on no sleep and knew there would be no rest anyway until they resolved this. He had called her at least ten times since Seth had left, but she hadn't picked up her phone. Then, it rang in his hands, just as he was about to attempt another try, and she told him simply to meet her at Sean and Jennie's.

Crisis counseling. She had gone there to get Sean and Jennie, with their perfect marriage, to do crisis counseling with them.

Stu would do it, he told himself again and again as he sped all the way over there. He would do anything at this point to get Abby to be okay with him, to be okay with them... to just be Abby.

The only crisis that greeted him when he arrived, though, was Abby, soaking wet in the bathroom where their nephews sat in the bathtub, gleefully splashing bubbles and suds everywhere. She managed a small, shy smile his direction when he walked in.

"Hey, Stu," she said.

"Abby," he murmured. "Abby, I'm sorry. I'm so sorry –"

And she cut him off as she stood up and pulled his face to hers, kissing him into silence.

As she broke away, she left him no silence to speak into. "Help me with the boys," she said quietly, handing him a towel. "Can you get Ezra?"

Stu just nodded numbly. He helped her to get both boys out of the tub, dried off, lotioned up, and back in diapers and clean clothes. He pulled on their socks as Abby brushed the fuzz on their heads, kissing them softly before she took them into the living room where Jennie had a toybox full of all the natural, holistic, educational toys she'd bought for them.

Abby pulled Stu down to sit next to her on the couch and curled into him, saying nothing at all.

Before he could apologize again for everything, to tell her that he would take her nowhere near a church that could hurt her as badly as she'd already been hurt, she told him, very simply, "They hurt my mother, too. They hurt her worse than they hurt him, honestly, because she... could never fight back. She would've become another problem he had to fix. So, she just had to hold it all in, to be who he needed her to be, to be who the church needed her to be... and she lost herself in that."

Stu pulled her closer, surprised that he'd never considered this part of the story before. "I didn't know," he said softly.

"You weren't there," she said. "How could you have known?" A pause as she relaxed into him. "She had... anxiety problems. Couldn't sleep at night. And he didn't get it. Didn't see what it had done to her. Kept telling her how she needed to be there for him, and... he didn't get it.

But that wasn't his problem, so much as it was hers, you know. Because if Christ had been to her who she said He was, she would've gotten through it. Through anything." She looked up at Stu, the tears now falling from her eyes. "And she did, didn't she? She got through it. She still believes, still loves Christ, even still, even after all that happened. So Jesus must have been who she said He was, even if it took that kind of refining in her to see Him as such."

She took a deep breath. "And He is who He was. And He will be who He says He is. And I can trust that."

Stu nodded. "We can trust that. We can trust Him. But Abby, if this is all just –"

Abby shook her head and blew out a deep breath. "But even with all of that baggage with my family... geez, *your* family is completely crazy, Stu."

He thought about this for a moment, wondering at the shift in the conversation, the places her mind was going this morning. "Well... yeah. Probably. Even with your family and their history... I still have the upper hand on insanity, don't I?"

She laughed a little at this, prompting him to smirk at her.

"And you don't know the half of it," she said. "Sean and Jennie? Are completely dysfunctional."

Stu made a face at this. "How so?"

"It's a long story, involving flatulence and fertility. And, no, I really don't want to explain that to you right now."

"Okay," he nodded, after a moment.

"And then, there's Scott. I'm going to be his wingman. Going to go around to bars, picking up women, pretending that I'm his crazy, psychotic wife if he needs me to."

Stu managed a small smile at this. "How... charitable of you."

She looked up at him, apology in her eyes. "I'm sorry that I said that about you earlier," she said.

"No, it's okay, it was —"

"And Sam," she sighed. "I mean, maybe he's sane, but after the way he climbed on top of the table at Christmas so as to better pound Scott in the face, even though he deserved it... well, I have my doubts about that. And Savannah was right there with him, holding Scott down, so. Well, you know."

"Yeah, I grew up with that," he nodded.

"And Seth!," she exclaimed. "Making out with Rachel!"

"Well, she was the one ripping his clothes off —"

"I didn't hear that part!," Abby gasped. "Though I can believe it."

"I told him to watch out for her," Stu said. "But that's because I'm a know-it-all who always tells people what to do, when to do it, how to do it, how to feel, and... crap, Abby. Are we okay? Will you forgive me?"

"No," she said, softly touching his face, reaching out and kissing him.

"You won't forgive me, but you'll still kiss me?," he asked.

"No," she said. "I mean that... no, *I* was wrong, Stu. Your whole family is crazy, this idea of yours is crazy, but... I'm just as bad. I went off on you without even considering that just possibly, the problem was really me."

He shook his head. "No, I wasn't listening to you —"

"And I wasn't listening to what you've been saying all along," she managed. "I got so caught up in what happened with my dad and my mother but... you aren't him. And I... I want to be like her, even if it hurts to get there. And it's not going to end up the same. And even if it did, Stu, even still, as long as we ended up together... it would be okay." She took a deep breath. "We should say yes. We should go forward. If this is what we're called to. And if you're called to it, we're *both* called to it."

"We can think it over," he began.

"You know what's right," she said softly. "I trust you. And I'm going to trust God." .

"Me and you," he whispered, tears in his eyes, as he held her face in his hands. "I'm not going to jeopardize that for anything. Because it's never God's call for me to be apart from you, Abby. The two of us. We'll come first, no matter what."

She sighed at this. "It's the three of us, Stu."

"The... what?"

"Stuart..." She sighed again. "I'm pregnant."

"What?," he gasped. "How did that happen?"

She gave him a look and couldn't hide her smile. "Really?"

"Well, I know how it... oh, wow..."

And she didn't say anything as he dropped to his knees before her, took her hips in his hands, and whispered, up against her jeans, "Hello in there..."

She could hardly see past her tears as he looked up at her. "Well, this changes a lot, doesn't it?"

She shook her head. "No. We're going forward. We'll say yes."

"Abby," he said softly, hope there in his eyes. "Are you sure?"

She swallowed back a sob. "No. But I'm going to trust God for whatever comes next."

CHAPTER EIGHT

Abby

It's four am, and I'm pretending to be asleep. I feign wonderfully comatose sleep when the baby starts to fuss, silently rejoicing when I feel the weight shift next to me in bed.

I can hear him tiptoe over to the bassinet that's been in our room for two months now, can imagine precisely how he looks as he lifts her up and whispers love to her.

I should feel guilty for letting him take the night shift... early morning shift, whatever-this-is shift, after such a long Sunday. There was the prayer meeting before the service, a baptism, a deacon's meeting, a potluck, another committee meeting, and then a surprise banquet, celebrating Stuart's five years of ministry at our little church, which is not so little anymore.

The *first* five years, Stuart whispered to me, as we cut the cake in the fellowship hall, and I smiled at him, glad to be where we find ourselves.

Life has been good here. God has been good. Even if there have been hard times, contentious moments, and very big challenges, which there have been, we have been overwhelmed, more often than not, by how good God has been in bringing us here.

Even now, in the stilled silence of the parsonage, I can't help but smile a little.

"Abby, I know you're awake."

Okay, so I'm smiling a lot. "Stu," I whisper, my eyes still closed, "I am not."

He laughs softly, reaching out his foot to push the mattress just slightly. "Are, too. But that's okay. I planned on taking care of Claire anyway so you could have the morning to yourself to get ready for work."

I yawn and look over at him. Almost six years of marriage, and even still, the sight of him in the morning, half-dressed, is a thrill. Even more so with our adorable infant on his chest. "Maternity leave is over too soon, you know," I murmur.

"You don't have to go back," he says softly.

"I know," I answer, sitting up, looking over at the clock. "But I've missed it. I've missed every bit of it. I'm ready to see all those sweet second graders again."

He smiles at this, kissing the baby's head as he rubs her back. She stretches under his hand, still so tiny and still so new that we can't tell who she looks like just yet. I suspect, though, that she'll be all Stu.

I'm okay with that.

"No tears today, then?," he asks.

"Maybe a few," I swallow. "But she'll be right across the street at Mrs. Smith's house. Mrs. Smith, who incidentally, told me just yesterday in Sunday school that I should come around at lunchtime to check on her."

"And to get a little bit of the pot roast I'm sure she already has in the slow cooker, hmm?" He raises his eyebrows at me.

"Benefit of small town living, huh?"

"Among other things," he nods. "Glad we'll all be within three blocks of one another."

"Exactly. And with Chance there as well, I'll be able to –"

And in answer to that statement, we hear the howling begin. At 4am.

"Oh, good grief, I'm going to kill Seth," I groan.

"Well, he is an idiot," Stu affirms. "Want me to handle it?"

"Nope, you stay here," I say, leaning over to kiss him... lingering there a little longer and pulling him a little closer than is wise, probably, given the immediacy with which our son's new puppy (courtesy of Uncle Seth, the idiot) is now howling and waking up the whole neighborhood.

"Abby," Stu groans, reaching out his free hand to pull me closer, just as I release him.

"Later, Pastor," I say, the word not even clogging in my throat these days, as I turn and make my way into the kitchen, where the makeshift kennel I've set up is full of bloodhound and boy.

Chance is so wrapped around the wrinkly, noisy dog that I can't hardly tell where one begins and the other ends. He's a miniature version of Stu, masculine and sweet combined perfectly, and I struggle to keep from smiling, even as I gently nudge him awake, prepared to give him a stern lecture about how boys are to sleep in beds and dogs are to sleep in the kitchen.

"Good morning, Mommy," he says, smiling up at me with sleep in his eyes and snuggling closer to the howling puppy, as though this is where he belongs.

"Chance," I say, "what have I told you about sleeping out here?"

"The puppy was so sad, though," Chance yawns. "Uncle Seth gave him four shots yesterday. And I heard him crying. I couldn't let him cry.

You don't let Claire cry."

"This is a dog. Not your sister," I say.

"He's so sweet, though," Chance says. "Uncle Seth told me that he might stop crying at night if he could hear a heartbeat, you know. So that's why I'm on the floor, so he can hear my heartbeat." A pause. "I may have to sleep here every night."

I sigh. "Thanks a lot, Uncle Seth."

"Yeah," Chance nods. "He said you were probably going to kill him –"

I gasp a little at the accuracy of this and at the surprise of hearing my four year old say it –

"– but I said you wouldn't kill him because you want him to marry your friend. Not Miss Rachel. But the other friend."

I narrow my eyes at him. So sharp, just like Stu. So quick to say what he's thinking, all the time, just like Stu.

Already so up in his Uncle Seth's business, just like Stu.

"Well," I sigh. "You're right about that. Does he want to marry my friend, too?"

"I don't know, Mommy," Chance says, his attention diverted to the puppy who is now sniffing around the kitchen looking for a place to do his business. "Girls are gross."

"No, dogs are gross," I say, pulling him up gently. "Chance, take the dog out into the backyard."

"Okay," he says, jumping up, self-important with this task appointed to him, calling the dog and marching out into the cold.

I watch him from the door. As big a man as he thinks he is at four, he's still my tiny boy, and even as I smile out at the backyard, watching him closely, Stu comes into the kitchen and wraps his arms around my waist as he stands behind me.

"It's later," he whispers, attempting to run his hands up underneath my shirt as he pulls me closer. "And the baby is asleep again."

"And Chance is out in the yard," I answer, holding him back by the wrists, smiling back at him. "Look at him."

He follows my eyes out to where Chance is motioning to the puppy, telling him what to do out in the cold yard.

"Doesn't he know it's four in the morning?," Stu murmurs, and I can hear the smile in his voice.

"Just following Uncle Seth's strict orders to spend every waking moment taking care of that dog," I say. "He's trying to get the puppy to go... oh, Stu! He's going to pee in the –"

And sure enough, Chance is now peeing right in big middle of the backyard, demonstrating to the puppy just what he's supposed to be doing.

"Good grief," I murmur, as Stu laughs out loud.

He's loud enough that Chance hears him. He turns and smiles our direction, waving enthusiastically. After the puppy finally does his business, Chance leads him in, high-fiving his father as he makes his way into the kitchen.

"Nicely done, man," Stu says.

"Who told you that it was okay to pee in the backyard?," I can't help but sputter.

Chance shrugs. "Uncle Scott said when a man's gotta go, a man's gotta go. We both peed into the pool at Grandma's house during Thanksgiving. He said he'd get me a cookie if I could aim and hit Uncle

Sean while he was talking on his cell phone."

"Did you?," Stu asks.

"Nah," Chance shakes his head. "But Uncle Scott did."

"Well, that sure does sound like Uncle Scott," Stu smiles. Then, he smiles even wider as he trades a look with me. "What?"

"He's no longer allowed around *any* of your brothers," I say.

"Fair enough. Hey, buddy, go wash your hands, and we'll start breakfast for Mommy, okay?," he says.

We watch him run full speed for the bathroom as the puppy runs after him, both of them all arms and legs.

"Pancakes?," Stu asks, smiling.

"Yeah," I sigh as I smile back. "It's early enough that I can help, though."

And it's quick work, as we go to it, as Chance comes back and Stu helps him up into a chair so that he can stand side-by-side with us, flipping the pancakes, adding the butter, smearing syrup all over the tops –

Claire wakes up again, and she can be put off no longer. Stu puts a hand to my arm, kisses my forehead, and makes his way to the bedroom, as I move to make a bottle and Chance carries the food to the table.

We move more efficiently these days. Chance has never known differently, but Stu and I have adjusted to life in the parsonage, life in the ministry, and we've changed in the process. There are schedules to make. Plans to check and recheck. Dates to remember. People to call, relationships to maintain, and even in our tiny town, new contacts to make.

Stu is discipling Shannon's husband. I'm teaching a ladies' study on restoration and forgiveness within the church. We're partnering with Sean and Jennie's church to help establish a multi-ethnic ministry two towns over. Our church is growing, and our people are being stretched. They weren't who they were. The church, this town, has been changed by Christ, and we…

… we've been changed as well.

I look up from where I stand at the sink, the bottle in my hand and tears in my eyes, as I see just a fraction of what God has done.

There's Stu, back in the kitchen now with Claire in one arm, his Bible laid out on the table in front of him, ready to read Scripture to our family before breakfast, even as Chance climbs up into his lap, still not too old for this closeness. Stu is just exactly who he was all those years ago, when I promised him forever, and yet he's so different. He's a pastor now, a father, and a man who finds fulfillment in what he does. He's certain to change even more as the years go by, as certain to change as Claire is, as Chance is…

… as I am.

And even still, we're us. I find I love him more than I did, that I know him better than I did, as God has knit us together over the years. We've changed together, grown together, and been covenanted together in the faithfulness of God, as we walk with Him into even the uncertain seasons of life.

It has been exponentially harder and infinitely better than I ever dreamt it would be back when he first spoke to me in the dorm hallway, all those years ago.

Stu senses my eyes on him and looks up, his arms full of children, and gives me his smile.

And I return it, making my way to his side, eager to begin whatever God has next for us.

ABOUT THE AUTHOR

Jenn Faulk is a full time mom and pastor's wife in Pasadena, Texas. She has a BA in English-Creative Writing from the University of Houston and an MA in Missiology from Southwestern Baptist Theological Seminary. She loves talking about Jesus, running marathons, listening to her daughters' stories, and serving alongside her husband in ministry. You can contact her through her blog www.jennfaulk.com

Made in the USA
Lexington, KY
13 June 2014